CASSANDRA CIELO

THE NIGHT, THE POWER
BOOK 2

Content Warning : There are depictions of violence and death. Heavy topics such as grief and loss. Though it is a closed door romance with no explicit scenes, there are some makeout scenes but characters do not go further than kissing on page.

MT. ARYTHMA
WYCLIFF
CITADEL
ORO
BEZER PLAINS
MT. ERAN
ERASMUS
MT. KIDRISOL
BLUE VOLCANO
N
E
W
S

COINANIA
TYNDALE
PALACE MOREH
KINGDOM OF SHAMAR
ROMATH
CASTLE JUDAHALL
KINGDOM OF GOLAN

CHAPTER 1

Lesson One: Let There Be Fire

The sun embraced the treetops, shining ribbons of gold through the encroaching night, as if a call to hope, even if things seemed without it now.

"You're falling asleep on the horse again."

I startled slightly as Shroding's voice filled my mind.

"I wasn't asleep," I protested, though my eyes had, in fact, been closed. Though I hadn't kept a normal schedule these last few months, I had still grown up on a farm. I was timed to rise and fall with the sun, and being with Shroding was the safest I had felt in months. With my body finally at peace it seemed to be reverting to old ways.

"How do you even manage that... with all the bouncing?" Shroding mused. He gestured towards where I was atop Etienne, whose hooves clopped steadily along the dirt path.

"I wasn't asleep," I insisted with a laugh, puffs of white plumed in the air with each of my breaths.

"Then have you taken up meditation?"

"I'm just resting my eyes. All these trees and more trees are giving me eyestrain." I closed my eyes again for emphasis.

"Nature could never give someone eyestrain." He deadpanned.

"Fine, fine, you win, I'm exhausted."

Etienne slowed to a stop beneath me.

A jolt of panic zipped through my chest—I was still skittish from all that had happened on the farm. There must be some danger that had caused us to halt. I opened my eyes, my panic turning to awe as before me spread a wide view of the western snowcapped mountains and the most beautiful sunset of watercolor pinks and teal blues.

"Wow," I breathed. Golden beams clung to the rock face as if the sun wasn't ready to let go just yet. I looked down at Shroding. *I know how you feel,* I thought in agreement with the sun. I had let go of a lot to be here, and though I did not regret my choice, I had not truly been ready for it either.

"What were you saying about trees?" Shroding teased, stepping into an errant pool of golden light. His fur refracted rainbows between the silvery strands.

I gazed at him with that strange sense of allegiance and wonder I had felt in the woods only last night, when I realized who he really was. The lost prince, the one born to save the world from Skithian. I was glad I was on Etienne because if I wasn't, I probably would have threaded my fingers through his fur in amazement as I had done so inappropriately before.

Distracting myself, I looked up at the fading light of day. It had been dawn when we left the farm... left Micah and the children, and now night was falling once more. Sorrow laced through my heart as I recalled the hurt on the kids' innocent faces as I rode away. The love in Micah's eyes, a love I didn't know how to return. And despite my effort all day not thinking about them, and all that had transpired, the moment

I did, bile rose in my throat. Denying the grief I was in did not make it go away.

I shivered as the silent autumn air snaked through my burned and tattered clothes, unforgiving in its chill. As unforgiving as the path my thoughts had gone down. I quickened Etienne's pace, eager to catch up to Shroding, who had moved nearly out of sight.

My stomach growled softly. It would be best to find a town or village where we could stay for the night and get supplies. It would be nice to have a coat for when the altitude brought snow down upon us, for no doubt it would soon, and the frayed remains of my mother's beige coat did very little against such an eventuality. But what towns were this deep into the mountains?

"Prince Shroding?" I called, my voice timid. "Shouldn't we be settling down for the night? Finding a town or something?"

He was quiet for a long moment. "No, I'm afraid that's not possible. It will draw unnecessary attention."

"Attention?"

"I don't think you want another experience like the one from last night, in the alley."

I stiffened, recalling the possessed men who'd attacked me outside the club. Their hollow purple eyes.

"You have no idea how..." He paused, his words a jumble as he struggled to find the right one to complete his thought. "... odd... you feel?"

I opened my eyes, which had closed to shut out the horrible memories of that night. "How I feel? Do you mean the king's power?"

"You emanate the strongest vibration to ever exist; even a novice with the gift would be able to sense that."

I was the novice, and after everything I had been through last night on the farm, I was the antithesis of strong right now. I recalled the peculiar way Thanes, Micah's friend, had looked at me in the club. He knew I hadn't carried the gift before, so had he sensed it that night?

"I can avoid crowds," I offered. The heaviness of the day's travels weighed on me, especially at the idea of sleeping on the ground with my side exposed in my torn dress. Self-consciously I pulled my beige coat over the revealed skin. I just wanted a shower and a warm bed.

"Wraiths tend to linger in towns, looking for bodies to inhabit. You would be in even more danger than you are right now."

"But—" I yawned.

"Can you trust me on this?" he clipped testily. I wanted to tell him I was starving, but I couldn't recall the last time I'd seen him eat. I imagined he was just as hungry as I was.

"Alright," I acquiesced, eyes falling closed as we sojourned on.

Sometime later Shroding spoke again.

"Stop here."

I cracked my tired eyes open, taking in the darkened path, the moon not yet high enough to illuminate the road. My legs were sore and body aching as I stretched my arms overhead, shaking off the short nap I had taken. Etienne stopped in front of a small cavern and spring. Steam rose from the surface of the water in the frigid mountain air.

A hot spring?

"Where are we?" I asked, dismounting clumsily like a baby fawn learning to walk. My legs were all pins and needles, and I leaned on Etienne as I waited for feeling to return to them.

"At the base of Corin." The smallest of the mountains in the range that stretched from Wycliff to Tyndale. "We will rest here tonight."

Gingerly I stretched my legs, trying to keep the side of my dress closed as I rolled my tight hips and throbbing lower back. When blood finally flowed to my toes again and the pins and needles stopped, I cleared my throat, which was still raw from the smoke inhalation.

"Is it safe?" I rasped, pointing at the pool of glorious steaming water.

"Yes." He nodded, tail flicking side to side. "Let it cool a little first if you decide to drink it." His voice was gentle as if he was afraid of being too loud or forthright. As if I were some frightened creature that at the slightest provocation would get on my horse and leave. Which I had no desire to do, in fact, by the way my butt muscles spasmed, I would be just fine not riding again for weeks. "I'll go get firewood," he informed me, disappearing into the brush.

It was my first time seeing a hot spring, and despite the heaviness in my heart, my curiosity had me a little bit excited, so much so that a smile split across my chapped lips. The sheer thought of getting the smoke stench off my body and soot out of my hair had me wanting to jump in, clothes and all. As if it could wash away all the memories of last night.

I inspected my clothes, the jagged rip along my side and the once pretty white lace, which was stained beyond recognition. Despite my wanting to jump in fully dressed, my clothes would have to keep smelling like smoke, as I did not have anything to change into while they dried. It was too cold to walk around in my underwear, nor did I feel comfortable doing so in front of anyone, especially the future king. At least my hair and skin would be clean. I stripped off the ruined layers, draping them over Etienne's saddle.

A twig snapped, and I jumped as Shroding dropped a small bundle of branches on the ground by the cave opening. Grabbing the beige coat and donning it, I tried to make my body small behind Etienne. But Shroding did not look my way. I guessed he knew where I was because he didn't even glance around for me either. He pushed the sticks with his nose till they leaned against each other, making a point. Curiously he stared at the pile.

"Where are you getting those stacks of wood?" I wondered, inching out from behind Etienne.

"I came here a few days ago and set up camp. I hid some firewood behind the cave." Holding the coat tightly closed around me, I moved to the mouth of the cave, where Shroding had dropped the bundles.

"How did you know I would come?"

"I didn't know, but I hoped." He ran back and forth a few more times to bring more wood from where he had stockpiled it.

I knelt, peering the kindling in the center of the sticks. How did he intend to light it?

When he bounded over, a moss-covered branch locked in his jaw, I asked as much.

After righting the branch next to the others, he said, "The vibration gift can be used to do many things."

I tilted my head, appraising the pile. It was said the gift could be used to make fire, wind, to bend water and more, as everything in the world has a vibration, but only those with honed skill and great power are able to do such things. I supposed the king would be one of those people.

"So are you going to light it?" I marveled, shuffling back a little as if the bundles of sticks would spontaneously burst into flames.

"No, I don't have the vibration gift in this form."

"You don't?"

He chuckled. "Of course not. You have the king's power, remember?"

I frowned, understanding clicking into place. The king's power was Shroding's vibration gift. Did that mean when he became human again the power would return to him?

"If you're not lighting the fire, then..." I trailed off, my hand lifting to point up at my face.

He gestured to the stack with his paw. "Haya?" His dark eyes flashed, watching expectantly. Puffs of white rose from his nose as he panted from running around in the frigid night.

My eyes widened. "I don't even know how to use the gift!"

"You used it three times before," he offered unhelpfully.

Four times actually, but I supposed he did not know about the time with Micah.

I held out my hands, a little desperate. "Yes, and each time it was in a moment of terror and high emotion. I haven't the first clue how to use it now."

He moved so he was at my side, ears perked and tail twitching.

"Then let me show you." He pushed his head against my hands till my palms cradled his whiskers, fingers under his jaw. I folded my knees under me, making myself level with him.

His fur was soft and warm, and I rubbed my thumbs over the bridge of his nose absently. His ever present purr grew louder when I was near.

He shifted closer, sitting in front of me, his tail tapping

my knee. "There are steps to training: first, you must learn the body movements. The way to feel and flow the power through you. That is how you wield it. It is called Krav, and every movement learned taps into one's power. I can't really show you the movements in this form, but I can help you with the meditation part. Meditation is what comes after learning Krav. This is when you begin to feel the power working through your body. You can move into the vibration dimension. Most can only stay in the vibration dimension a short time, as it requires immense concentration."

Wait, another dimension? Just how many were there? "Is it like the dimension I go into when I sleep?" I asked.

"No, it's very different. The only senses there are sight and sound. You can see and hear the vibrations of the world around you, but the world itself is black except for the color each living thing gives off. Every living thing—grass, trees, bugs, people—has a distinct color and emits a distinct sound."

"I can't really imagine it."

"That's okay, you don't have to imagine it, you will see it." His tail stilled, draping over my knees. "Now, shall we practice?"

"What do I do?" I laughed nervously.

"Close your eyes first," he ordered, a chuckle in his voice as well. "Breathe easy, focus on my pulse, where my jaw and neck meet. Listen for it, feel it against your fingers."

The rhythmic thrum was hard to pinpoint against the constant rolling of his purr, but when I targeted the sensation against my hands I latched on to it.

"Imagine that pulse like a string flowing from me to you."

I did. I tried to imagine the string stretching between us, the vibration dimension around us, but nothing happened. I waited, my eyes closed, my thoughts as quiet as I could make them. After a moment I sighed. "Nothing, I'm getting nothing." It couldn't be as easy as just thinking about a thing and believing it would happen, could it?

"You're trying too hard. You can do this. Don't be afraid of the gift. Trust it."

I sat quietly for a while, expecting something to change inside me, but I still felt the same, except the cold had gotten worse, and I shivered. My thoughts wandered to the hot spring a few feet away, and I wanted to be curled up in that warmth instead of kneeling in front of a nonexistent fire.

"You are too distracted."

I jumped a little and then glared. "Well, then let me focus," I retorted.

"Take deep breaths. Listen to the quiet around you. It's when you let go of trying to control your surroundings that you will start to feel them."

I sighed. Squaring my shoulders and sitting up properly, I focused on the gentle thump of Shroding's pulse. I timed my breathing to it. In and out. Listened as the rise and fall of the breeze joined in unison. Each intake of breath and exhalation was like falling, and a completely different kind of shiver passed down my spine.

"Feel the world around you expand, in the same way that when you breathe in, your shoulders push away from each other." Shroding's voice was soft, almost far away.

Hundreds of tiny pinpricks patterned over my fingertips, in time with his pulse. A sharp but warm sensation followed and spread through my hands, which still held his jaw.

Like every other time, a mix of fear and excitement warred inside me as the gift rippled up my arms to my chest. Warmth coursed through my body, which was too small a container for the yawning heat and trembling inside.

"Now take all of it and funnel it out of you through my pulse. Through the string between us."

Though I wanted to question it, I pushed away my doubts and tried to do what I was told. The energy inside me reminded me of the evening sun when it hit the expanse of golden wheat on the farm. How the whole valley would shine, radiating golden light. I imagined Shroding's pulse to be the sun, reabsorbing its light, and my body the wheat letting go of the light, giving way to the night, to being empty.

Shroding whimpered. And what sounded like an oil lamp being set ablaze whooshed between us. A loud crack and pop suffused the air with a burst of heat.

CHAPTER 2
I Think He Knows

My eyes flew open, landing on a small flame that licked up the kindling, drawing in the fuel of wood and leaves to grow stronger. I watched in amazement as the fire smoldered.

"I did it?!" I marveled as Shroding pulled his head away, body swaying. "How did I do it?" I shook my head, wondering where the fire had come from if I hadn't even thought about it.

"You did great," Shroding said as he curled down next to the fire.

"Hey, are you okay?" I worried, seeing a dullness in his eyes that hadn't been there before.

"I'll be fine."

My brow knit. "That wasn't all me, was it?" I accused. "What did you do?"

"To make fire requires immense control. All this is still new to you, so I used myself as a conduit, connecting your power to the focus needed to make fire." He sounded weak.

"But it hurt you."

"It doesn't feel great, I'll admit that much."

I narrowed my eyes in the universal glare that said I wanted a better explanation.

"The power wants to come back to me, that's the only reason I can be a conduit for it, but this body is not made for such power," Shroding mumbled. "It's been a very long time since I've had vibrations move through me, let alone one so vast as the king's power." His breath puffed out shallow and unsteady. "It will pass."

I supposed I had no choice but to take his word for it. There were so many things about the gift, about his world I did not understand. Still, I was grateful for the fire and for the lesson Shroding had taught me. There was so much I could do with the gift, and I was somewhat surprised to realize I very much wanted to learn.

As the fire curled around the stacks of wood, it illuminated the opening of the cave. Inside was a bedroll, a canteen and a worn leather pack.

"What is this?"

I shuffled over and opened the leather pouch. Rolled into the bag were my work pants and my warmest sweater, a thick green wool one my mom had bought for me while she was visiting the capital a few years ago. I rummaged through the bag, finding food and a blanket.

"I packed a few things I thought you might need." Shroding lifted his head a little, the movement seeming to take a lot of effort. He had overextended himself, and not just from the use of the vibration gift a moment ago. He had not stopped moving since we left the farm. His fur was singed from the fallen rubble that had pinned him during the fire at the farmhouse, and his paws were cracked and bleeding from the craggy terrain of the mountain trail. "I figured you would come back from your date with some idea of what was going on and... well, since you had told me to be ready..." He trailed off, resting his head, eyes closing, ears folding back. I blushed, seeing he had also packed my undergarments.

"Thank you," I mumbled, mortified but more grateful than words could express. "How did you get all the way here, set this up and still get back in time to save me from those possessed men?" How had he even known I had been in danger? Had he been able to hear me calling to him?

Shroding's eyes were still closed as he lay on his side, which rose and fell with deep, even breaths. Was he asleep? I took the canteen and filled it with water from the spring, busying myself as I waited for his response, or no response at all if he had actually fallen asleep, which I would not fault him for.

After a moment his voice filled my mind. "I had set up most of this a few days back. I only brought the pack that night. We took the trails to get here, as Etienne would not have been able to follow the path I took on my own. In a straight shot, we are only a few hours away from Wycliff."

Finding the water in the canteen cool, I knelt at his side, my fingers brushing along his fur. His dark eyes opened and watched me. I found the burns and cuts that patterned his back. Gently I used the cooled water to clean his fur and wash out the wounds.

He flinched at my ministrations, eyes blinking slowly with pain.

"You don't have to do that." He hummed in my mind.

"They could get infected." I dismissed his protest, and focused on washing away the flecks of blood and soot.

"I've had worse but... thank you," he murmured, body relaxing into the ground wearily. I shifted closer, reaching over him to access and clean his paws. It was only when my coat peeked open at my thigh that I remembered I was not wearing anything save for the ruined coat.

"How did you know where to find me? When the wraiths attacked me in the alley?"

His tail twitched, and he purred, claws extending as he flexed the pads of his feet. "The king's power in you calls to me. It wants to be reunited... with me."

"I tried calling you." I tapped the side of my head. "In my mind. I thought that's how you knew I was in trouble."

From the tone of his voice, I imagined if he were human, he would have been smirking. "It certainly affirmed it for me." His claws retracted and ears twitched. "But no, I sensed your fear, sensed the king's power the moment you tried to use the gift. I had already gotten back to the farm by then, so it did not take long for me to get to you."

So he had heard me? Had he heard me the other times I had spoken to him?

"What do you mean you *felt* my fear?"

"The power has linked us, mind, body..." He trailed off, staring at the flames. "It's why I can speak to you, here and in the other dimension."

So then only I could communicate with him?

"Then can you always hear my thoughts, feel what I'm feeling? It seemed as though you tried to talk to me a few times, but I usually only hear my name."

"Yes, I can sometimes hear your thoughts, and I meant it when I said you were not listening before. As much as you might have wanted to understand all that was happening to you, your subconscious did not want to let me in. I have to focus and you have to listen for us to communicate. The closer we are, the easier it seems to be. I tried to tell you a few times who I was, but you weren't ready to hear it."

Seemed simple enough, and yet we had missed hearing each other so many times. I would need to try harder to listen but also be more cautious of what I thought about and felt around him. I already had felt and thought—by the Strings, even *said*—such absurd things in his presence. How much had he overheard? Mortification filled me, and I watched to see if he could sense the emotions in me now.

He let out a puff of air. "Your emotions, on the other hand, those come at me with no filter. I can feel you more than I can hear you. It's rather frustrating, knowing you have an emotion but not understanding the thoughts behind it."

I chewed my lip. "So you can feel *all* my emotions, regardless of whether it's intentional?"

He lifted his head, gaze unwavering as he looked at me. "I feel you... all the time. From the very first moment you touched me on the dandelion hill."

Heat burned my neck and cheeks. I had thought his voice in my head an intrusion, but now not even my emotions were my own. He knew every time I felt terror, joy, guilt and even lust. My chest sank as I recalled the kiss Micah and I had shared in the hallway, the one Shroding had interrupted. By the Strings! Those moments were private, personal, and to have someone, anyone, let alone the future king privy to those feelings was like standing naked against my will and being judged for it. Shame pooled in my belly like hot acid.

Shroding shifted, lifting onto his front paws and leaning forward till his fur brushed my cheek and his neck hugged mine in a strange embrace.

"I'm sorry."

My shoulders stiffened. "Why are you sorry?"

"It is unfair that I should feel all your emotions and yet mine are closed off to you. I realize it is merely the avenue for the king to protect the power, but it is terribly one-sided. Please know I would not judge you for any emotion of yours I have ever felt."

I shook my head, pulling away. "Thank you for that."

"Actually I should thank you."

"R-Really, why?"

"I have been trapped as a cat for two hundred years, and, well, through you I have experienced emotions I had not been able to even recall for some time. It was confusing at first. I didn't know where the feelings were coming from, but once I understood they were yours, it became rather exciting to me. In some ways it was like being a child again and experiencing everything for the first time, after so many years without feeling much of anything."

"You're welcome, I guess." I turned my head towards him, smirking a little, knowing I would probably regret asking but curious all the same. "Is there a particular emotion that stood out?"

His dark eyes flashed. "A few, but..." He nudged my shoulder with his head, gaze falling to the exposed skin of my upper thigh. "You ought to clean up, and get some rest. We really do have a long journey ahead."

I would have blushed had not this whole conversation maintained the burning flush across my neck and face. Carefully I crossed my arms in a pout as a way to discreetly pinch my coat closed.

He must think I'm very brazen to have had this whole conversation in nothing but a tattered coat. When he said nothing else and closed his eyes, I stood, taking the fresh clothes with me over to the spring.

I dug a hole, lining it with rocks, and filled it for Etienne to drink from. With my back to Shroding, I removed my coat, sinking into the warm water. I covered my mouth, squealing with delight as the warmth did wonders for my tight muscles. Squeezing my eyes shut, I submerged my head, savoring the rush of heat across my scalp. When I surfaced, the cold mountain air had me shivering deliciously.

Sighing, my skin flushed and body content, I dreamed of staying in the hot spring forever.

CHAPTER 3

Palace Moreh

After a while I could feel Shroding's gaze on the back of my head. I turned as his voice filled my serene mind.

"You're going to pass out if you keep sitting in there," he said, and for the first time since we set out on this journey, his voice held a lightness that made me sure he was teasing me.

I almost stood to face him, then remembered I was in fact naked in the water. It was too easy to forget he was a man behind the cat's exterior. Not just any man, an amazingly gorgeous prince. I mean, by the Strings, he was the prince of Shamar! I swallowed hard, wondering how I would deal with the strange feelings I had developed for him in the other dimension.

"Oh," I gasped, water splashing violently about as my hands covered my traitorous mouth. I had kissed the prince of Shamar. No, I had literally thrown myself at him.

I sank into the water, my heart racing. If only disappearing was an ability of the king's power. He could have me beheaded or thrown in prison for assault. I panicked for a few moments, not actually sure if he would do something like that.

He moved towards the spring, his silver fur catching my attention. The firelight glinted in his onyx eyes.

"What is going on in that mind of yours?" His dark gaze scrutinized me.

"What?" I squeaked, dizzy from the heat—definitely from the heat.

"Listening now? I have been trying to tell you that you should eat something and rest, before you actually pass out from the heat." His voice sounded a little amused. Did he know what I'd been thinking? Had I left myself open to him? I would need to learn how to use the power inside me, and fast. Not just to bring him back, but also to keep my thoughts and feelings private when I wanted to.

"Turn around," I whispered.

"As you wish." He turned his back to me, and I was certain he could feel my embarrassment.

"Don't even think about looking," I added, doubting very much he would be interested anyway. I leapt out, grabbing the fresh clothes. Taking a few seconds, I savored the feeling of clean garments against clean skin. I jumped and tugged, struggling to get the clothes over my wet skin. When I was decent, he turned around and nudged the bag of food.

I frowned, holding my wet, tangled hair.

"What's wrong?"

"I don't have a brush..." I trailed off, starting to finger comb the long tresses. Tomorrow my hair would be a frizzy, wild mess, and if I tried to braid it like this, I would have so many tangles it would be better to cut it off. Though it shouldn't, something about that thought was like one step too far. After everything, the idea was just too much, and I slumped to the ground next to the spring. I had lost everything, but this small thing cracked open the floodgates I had been determined to keep locked up.

"Haya." He came over to me, his dark eyes observing my tears with an unreadable expression.

"I'm fine, it's fine." I rubbed my eyes, wishing the unbidden wave of grief would stop.

"It's not so bad, it's just hair, right?" He gestured to his fur, which was matted in some spots, clearly not brushed in a very long time. How had I never noticed? "Come on." He walked to the mouth of the cave, and I followed, breathing deeply to stop the tears.

I sat on the bedroll, taking a hunk of bread and biting it. Like most things the last few weeks, it tasted like ash in my mouth. Still I ate it.

Swallowing the crust and the lump in my throat, I hedged, "Can I ask you a question?" I licked my lips, the morsel gone as hunger won out over flavor.

"Anything," he answered, looking absently at the fire.

"Can the Wraiths..." I paused, worrying my lip, unable to stop the shaky sniff that accompanied the tears that burned my eyes. I would not cry again.

"You are safe. The Grieving move terribly slow, bodies decaying and such. They are at least two days behind us, and the Wraiths need someone with the gift to possess. They can't possess you since you have the king's power, and they can't use me, as I'm..." He flicked his tail in a gesture towards his animal form.

I nodded, taking a long swig of water, my throat still raw from the smoke. My mind wandered to Micah. Was he too drinking water to relieve the scratching pain? Had the children all gotten treatment? Were they feeling better tonight? I downed the rest of the canteen, wishing I could know for sure that they'd all made it home safe.

"What about when I move between dimensions?"

"I won't let anything happen to you. Just call for me." His dark eyes turned to me, and in them I could almost see the prince looking back. The promise of protection in those eyes was enough to relax my shoulders and loosen the knot in my stomach.

"I have a lot of questions. Some I don't even know how to ask."

"I know. Sleep now, we can talk more soon. We have a long road ahead of us."

"You said that before—where are we going exactly?"

"To Palace Moreh."

That name was so familiar. I closed my eyes briefly, exploring all the trade maps burned into my mind from years on the farm, till I recalled where I knew that name from.

"That is the summer palace, in Tyndale?"

"Yes, that is our destination." His head rested heavily over his paws as he lay next to the fire.

I looked at my hands. What was I supposed to do with the king's power when we got to the palace? I had dreamed of the throne room only a few nights back, and that seemed like the more prudent place to go. Why Tyndale and not Castle Judahall in the capital? The prince would be safer in a castle protected by his armies than some vacation-home palace.

"I know I said I would go wherever you lead me, but"—fiddled with the ends of my hair—"why are we going there?"

"Haya..." He sounded exasperated. "Aren't you tired?"

"Oh, umm, I guess all those naps on Etienne were restful." I rubbed the back of my neck, chagrin.

His responding laugh was soft, almost relenting in timbre.

"Of course they were," he said as if he were talking to a child, which to him, I suppose I kind of was.

As if to prove the point, the moonlight spilled into the clearing, no longer obscured by the clouds above. The light turned Shroding's silver fur into that impossible shade of amethyst. My chest squeezed, and a longing to be closer to him had me scooting till my hip was flush with his back.

Again, as if my hands had a mind of their own, they threaded through his fur, his purring in rhythm with the crackling fire. Were there ever two sounds more soothing? My whole body wanted to melt onto the bedroll next to him, and hold his body next to mine like a pillow, as I had done so many times before at the farm. By the Strings, what was I thinking! This was the prince, not Iri, not some pretend dream guy, but a real living, breathing human, albeit in cat form. Shocked by my dangerous thoughts, I withdrew my hands from his glowing fur and gave my own tresses a quick yank to clear my thoughts.

"So, why are we going to Tyndale?" I whispered, forcing my attention to the stars that peeked out of the dark sky above. Trying very hard not to look at him and feel that pull once more.

As if he somehow knew the power his glowing fur had over me, he rolled on his side, till most of his body lay in my shadow, returning a majority of his fur to its glossy silver. "It's where it all began for me. As a cat, that is."

"At the palace?"

"That is where I was changed." He closed his eyes and took a deep breath, the fur of his upturned side puffing up with the inhale. "It isn't too far from here. By horseback it's about a week's journey. We are making good progress so far." He pressed his paws into the side of my leg as he twisted to stretch, and despite myself I looked down at him. It was so cute, the way he arched his back, like any other cat. I almost giggled but caught myself. It seemed rather unforgivable to giggle at the future king.

"So you're thinking that to become human again you have to be there?"

"I know I do." He exhaled sharply, eyes still closed, body still bent in the long stretch. "My father would not have brought me all the way there for the first transformation if it could have been done at the castle in Romath."

"I suppose that makes sense." I brushed my hand along his fur, the temptation too great to resist, as his position had moved him back into the moonlight.

He lifted his head, and I could see in the way he curled up again in my shadow how tired he really was. I scratched gently behind his ears, I could ask more later. He needed rest too. But before I could say as much, he said, "Tell me what else is on your mind?"

"I was wondering about the dimension you are in..."

He took in my perplexed look. "Hm. How familiar are you with the different dimensions?"

I tilted my head, chewing my lip. "You mentioned the vibration dimension before."

"A few dimensions exist, ours and the vibration dimension being just two. For the sake of this explanation I'll just be talking about the spirit dimension; that is where I am. Just like the vibration dimension, which one learns to access when training their gift, it is a separate plane of our world. Normally the spirit dimension can only be accessed by the king, or in your case the king's power."

I nodded. So far his explanation seemed sound. Besides, I was accepting all kinds of things lately. The savior of our world being trapped as a cat being the most ludicrous one. Still, I grappled for a reference point. "So is it like how the Seraphs moved through time?"

"Yes, it is similar. However, you have not been to the actual spirit dimension. When you sleep, you unconsciously move into a rip inside the spirit dimension. The rip is where the Wraiths exist in their true form. That is why you can see the shadows there. In our world they are formless and need to possess in order to have any physical effect on things."

"If the spirit dimension is only accessed by the king, then how are the Wraiths there?"

"The Wraiths exist because of Skithian, whose power made the rip in the spirit dimension. He made it as a place for his Wraiths to live. Skithian's power is a counterpart to the king's. A darkness formed from distorting the gift the Creator of Strings gave to the king."

I scratched my head, loosely understanding what he was saying, but having many more questions. Like how had Skithian even gotten access to the king's gift in order to distort it? If the rip still existed, did that mean Skithian still had power? Why did I enter the place where the Wraiths were and not just the spirit dimension? "So I travel inside the rip Skithian made for the Wraiths?" I clarified.

He purred, eyes lighting up, pleased that I seemed to be understanding him. "That is correct."

"Why there? I mean, it would be safer for the king's power to be..." I lifted my palms. "...literally anywhere else."

"The king's power is looking for me, and gets you as close as it can to where I am."

"So you are in the rip as well? Is that why the Wraiths disappear when you show up?"

"Excellent question. When we are together, we are not in

the rip. We are in a pocket of the rip within the spirit dimension."

This time I blinked and shook my head, not understanding.

"Let me show you."

CHAPTER 4

Age Is But A Number

He nudged my hand with his head as he stood up. I followed him over to the hot spring. "Imagine this water as the spirit dimension." He gestured over the surface. "Now the rip is like..." He trotted over to a pile of rocks and pawed them till they fell into the shallow part of the pool, making a smaller separate pool. "...this. The rip is part of the whole but removed. You enter here." He pointed to the rip. "When I show up, you move into..." He paused, glancing around, and with his teeth pulled the purple flower of a weed, then dropped it into the smaller pool. "When I show up, you move into the flower with me. A pocket within the rip."

"And this pocket is safe from the Wraiths?" I asked, appreciating his visual aid.

He placed his paw over my hand and nodded. I drank in his reassurance, desperate to believe I was safe.

I sighed. "Everyone back in Wycliff is safe too? Now that I'm not there, because the Wraiths are after me," I reasoned.

He nodded, his expression burdened. "Yes, they want to stop you from helping me, and the easiest way would be to kill you." He flexed his paw, claws coming out and retracting. "Before you ask another question, let me explain what I do know. My father, the late King Roark, saved my life centuries ago, but in doing so he died. From what I read in your history book, it says he died and the war stopped, but that is not what really happened." His eyes darkened, and he looked away. "My mother was prophetic. She had many prophecies in her lifetime, and from what I was told, the last one claimed I would destroy Skithian once and for all. This knowledge terrified the dark spirit enough to seek out the king to make a deal. Skithian promised to end the war, forever, to stop corrupting the people and be locked away, but only if my father killed me. The king... agreed to the deal with Skithian. My life in exchange to save hundreds of thousands of innocents."

"Shroding, I—"

His ears flattened solemnly, but he continued. "My father had another plan in mind. He deceived Skithian. Instead of killing me, he used the king's power to change me into a cat and then hid my Nephesh, my soul, within a pocket tucked within Skithian's rip. Like with any great use of power, there is a cost. Using the king's power the way he did... it killed him. Skithian believed it was the grief of murdering his own son that caused my father to die. No one, except a select few, knew what really happened, and so I was erased. It was easy enough to do, as very few even knew I existed to begin with."

I recalled my history book and the change Micah had pointed out to me this year. Shroding may have been a myth all this time, but someone was clearly trying to prove he was real now. They were trying hard, enough to change the history books... but why now?

I tucked those questions away for later. "It must have been hard for you to know he sacrificed himself for you."

"It was for a long time, but I understand why he did it. He did not believe Skithian would keep his end of the deal. Skithian may have agreed to be sealed away in another dimension, as there are many, but he never would have stayed that way for long. My father needed me to stop Skithian and end this war, so I think I was his real plan all along. The long game, as they say nowadays. I was the only one who could do it—at least that's what the prophecy said."

"Couldn't he have had another child? Wouldn't the prophecy apply to them?"

"No, the prophecy was for the child of Elina and Roark. When she died it prevented another child from being born and fulfilling the prophecy."

"I see..." I nodded, contemplating. "So you said you became a cat when your father passed. How old were you?"

He stiffened slightly. "I was thirteen."

"Right, thirteen... umm, how long had you been thirteen?"

"Nearly ten of your years."

"Hmm." I pondered, chewing my lip. "Right, umm..." I scratched one finger behind my ear. "I don't get it." I deadpanned. "How old are you? You look my age."

He glanced down, flicking the surface of the water with his paw. "About four hundred years old now, I guess." His tail twitched, a sign of his discomfort. "Biologically around eighteen or nineteen, it was hard to keep track in the last two hundred years or so."

"F-Four hundred." I gaped. That was a lot more than the

forty-four Micah said he had lived, and forty-four had seemed like far too many. But would there have been a number I wouldn't have balked at? Probably not.

"I am part of the king's court, we age... differently."

"Yeah, I kind of figured that much out, but how does that work?" I finally asked.

"Ah, the real question," he clipped, taciturn. "When the Creator of the Strings gave my father this world, he gave our bloodline an unusually long life. Those in the king's court, those worthy, are given the same ability by the king himself. Only the king can give it and take it away."

"But how does it work? Are you like a baby for thirty years or something?"

Shroding laughed deep and full, temperament shifting. "By the Strings, no, that would be ghastly. I assure you it's nothing like that. But it is a secret only those in the court are allowed to know," he answered imperiously.

"Fine, but the king can take the magic aging away?"

"Magic aging?" He laughed again, making my cheeks heat. I was doing my best to understand, and he was laughing at me. I crossed my arms petulantly. "Magic is simply what we call things we can't explain, so, sure, magic, if that helps you wrap your mind around it."

I stuck my tongue out mentally.

"The king is the only one who can take it away, but a person can choose to give it up," he added after calming down.

To live hundreds, even thousands of years... why would someone want to give that up? Then I recalled Micah and his mom having given it up because they wanted to age normally with Misha. Why had Misha been born without the special aging?

"Does it usually extend to one's family?"

"Only immediate family, parents and children, but once the children marry they no longer have it. Otherwise there would be a lot of really old young people walking around."

I laughed a little, then sobered, thinking of Micah's father. Though I knew people with the court's long life could die—like Mr. Ilsan, the queen and king had—I still asked. "So do you just live forever?"

I could hear the smirk in his voice as he explained. "Not really. We can live a very long time. My father was four thousand when he died, which is much older than the average hundred and twenty those without the 'magic aging' can live." His tone grew serious as he continued. "After a while we do die. Old age is no respecter of persons, and of course we can be killed like anyone. I will pass from old age if I'm not killed earlier."

I flinched at his words.

I was not okay with the direction the conversation had taken. The last thing I wanted to think about was Shroding dying, especially when I was doing everything I could to make him human again.

There was something comforting about knowing he would be our king for a long time, long after my life was spent. That I would not have to see him pass.

"In the time I've been gone, I'm sure many in my father's court have left this world."

"So as the king, do you live the longest?"

"The ability stems from my bloodline, so it's strongest in me and any family I might have in the future."

An image of little Shrodings played through my mind, making me smile, then my eyes widened at the flutter that image gave my insides. I clapped my hands, trying to relax.

"You said you were erased but there were people who knew about the transformation?"

He glanced over at me, eyes scrutinizing. "I didn't know I was erased until recently. Until I saw how undeniably flummoxed you were at the mention of my name." He seemed tired suddenly, like telling these fantastical tales was draining for him. "But I shouldn't have been surprised, I have always been somewhat of a secret. When I was born, it was not announced to the kingdom. I grew up in hiding. My father knew the prophecy and what it meant for our world, and he was determined to keep me safe until it was time for me to fight back. I was only allowed three friends growing up and had my own secret passages in and around Castle Judahall. I didn't realize the whole world didn't know me. The only people who mattered knew I existed. I suppose everyone else who met me just assumed I was the kid of someone working in the castle."

"Did your friends know who you were, about you becoming a cat?"

"My friends did know I was the prince, but the only people who knew my father's plan were his general, commander and the head of the court. They were there when I... changed."

"Where are they now?"

"I don't know," he said softly, shifting to stand. He walked over to fidget with a nearby leaf hanging on a tree.

He was like me; fidgeting when talking about something that made him uncomfortable. I stood to walk over to him, thinking about how he was precious, protected. An asset kept from the world till the right time. A light for the darkest of times. I recalled how, each time he had saved me in the rip, the dimension had transformed before my eyes. From complete darkness to light. The sun always shone brightly overhead when he was there. The fear and heaviness from the Wraiths would vanish.

I glanced at Shroding, who was watching me approach. Was that what he was? A bringer of light, of power and salvation? How had I of all people been tasked with saving someone so important? It seemed like a terrible error, a plan gone awry.

Shroding's ears twitched, and his head jerked towards the ridge on the other side of the camp through the trees. "Someone's coming."

"I thought the Grieving were days behind us?" I panicked, kneeling next to him.

"They are."

His eyes scanned the woods, seeing far better than me in the pitch-dark night.

"The Wraiths, then? Did they possess someone, a hunter or traveler?" I wondered aloud.

Shroding growled, fangs bared. At the sight, adrenaline spiked through my core. "No, this is something far worse."

A figure, which appeared very human, passed through the trees below the ridge.

"Worse?" I questioned. What could possibly be worse than the Wraiths or Grieving? Skithian, I supposed, but I banished that thought. Skithian was long gone. Right?

"He was drawn by the smoke of the campfire," Shroding reasoned, glancing up at the moon. For the moment the clouds covered the revealing light, but we didn't know how long that would last.

"You need to hide, no one can see your fur!" I pushed against his side. Who knew if the prophecy in the yellow journal, from back at the farm, was in any of the king's other journals.

"My sentiments precisely." He bristled but didn't move.

"I'll take care of it," I promised, urging him in the direction of the cave, assuring him with a smile that I would be fine.

He flattened his ears, not buying it. With eyes narrowed at the approaching figure, he turned and slunk inside the cave, out of the moonlight and into shadow, voice filling my mind as I stood to face the intruder. "I'll stand down for now, but as I told you before, I won't let anyone harm you."

CHAPTER 5

Lesson Two: Appearances Are Deceiving

The scrape of a sword being drawn had my blood running cold. Still, I squared my shoulders and walked close to the fire, letting its light illuminate my face for the man to see.

He came through the brush, and once the light hit him, a look of surprise reshape his features.

"Miss?" He had not expected to see someone alone, especially a girl? His grip on his sword slacked as he straightened from the Krav fighting stance those in the military learned in order to wield their gift. He wore a Krav suit as dark as the night around us, but over top were metal adornments similar to those of the man who'd delivered the notice of death for my father and brother. The king's crest was etched sharply over the chest plate. The lion-like beast with four wings was poised to fight, as if it could launch from the breastplate and sink its fangs into the enemy. The gold linework caught the light, making the beast seem to be dancing with the flames.

I raised my hands to signal I was unarmed. He drew

closer, his expression softening as he assessed I was not a threat, and though he sheathed his sword, his eyes were shrewd. Judging from the bracers on his arms, he was of a high rank in the military. General, or commander? So where was his army? Was he traveling alone?

"Are you alone?" His voice was rough, lower than Shroding's, more raw, as if he was often yelling orders.

I nodded, my gaze finally lifting and settling on his face. I had intended to keep my gaze downcast as a show of respect, but his voice had me curious. He had long honey hair that brushed his shoulders, past a broad jaw, sharp nose and eyes that danced with the flames as much as the crest on his breastplate did. I shivered. He did not look that much older than me, so how did someone so young advance so quickly in rank?

He stopped a few paces away, the fire separating us like a boundary neither of us wanted to cross. He looked vaguely familiar, like I had seen him somewhere before, but that was highly unlikely. I didn't know many soldiers.

"You have seen him—I showed you his face, from one of my memories." Shroding's voice answered my unspoken question as the man before me also spoke, but I was too distracted to hear him. Instead I responded in my mind to Shroding.

"What do you mean? Who is he?" And better yet, what reason did I have to fear him?

"I'll explain more later, but his name is Callum, and as of right now I'm not sure if he can be trusted."

I swallowed thickly, wishing I had a weapon to defend myself with.

"Haya, breathe. He has no doubt sensed the vibration power in you, but he might not understand it to be the king's power. Whatever you do, don't use it. If you do, he will definitely be able to tell."

The soldier—no, Callum—turned and began to walk away, but I had not been paying attention to the words he spoke. Had he asked me a question?

"What?" I called to his back.

He looked at me over his shoulder, hand falling on the hilt of his sword, unimpressed by my lack of attention. He was clearly not used to repeating himself. "I said I will take you to a nearby village, these mountains are not safe," he repeated.

"No!" I shook my head. "I mean, no thank you, I came here to camp." I gestured to the bedroll beside the fire. "Besides, I can handle some wild animals." I gave a smile, hoping it was convincing, even as my traitorous fingers fidgeted with the ends of my hair.

"Wild animals are not the only things to fear in these woods."

My smile wavered. "I do not need your assistance."

Just as I had done, Callum had not looked directly at me since entering the clearing, though on my part it had been as a sign of respect. For him it had been to scan the trees, assessing threats, gaze flitting across my camp, taking in the hot spring, my damp hair, the remnants of my ruined clothes, which I had thrown into the fire to burn, tallying all the details behind his fathomless eyes. When those eyes finally met mine, my stomach lurched. He was way too handsome, and just like Shroding, his eyes seemed to have far more decades in their depths than his physical appearance let on.

Callum squared himself, holding my gaze as he took a step towards me, testing the unspoken boundary.

"Are you running from someone..." His hand remained

comfortably on the hilt at his hip, and I struggled to find the right words to quell his distrust. "... or, perhaps, something?"

He wouldn't attack me, right? I mean, he was a soldier. Then again, that sentiment meant little after being attacked in the alley back home. More importantly, Shroding knew him but did not think he could be trusted.

"I don't see how my business is any of yours," I snipped.

"You look of age, yet you're not training to fight in the war? Are you running from enlistment?" He raised an eyebrow, testing me.

"I-I—" What could I say? I had the gift, so of course he would assume I was training for enlistment, just as the men in the alley had. I had to lie. Unfortunately for me, I was terrible at lying.

"Tell him you are going to the garrison in Oro at first light," Shroding offered. Oro was in the direction of Tyndale, so it was not a complete lie, though after what Shroding said about the dangers of going to towns or cities, I didn't think he actually planned for us to stop there.

"I leave at first light for Oro." I crossed my arms, giving what I hoped was my best defiant attitude.

"I see." Callum lifted his chin. "Then as a fellow soldier I'm sure you would not mind if a commander joined you by the fire tonight?"

"You want to stay *here*?" I balked, arms out to my sides to encompass the small camp in question.

"I will escort you on your way tomorrow." His hand lifted from the hilt, and he began to remove his chest plate.

"I couldn't possibly inconvenience you so." I backpedaled.

"Not at all, I'm going a similar way, and as I said there are far worse things in these woods than wild animals. I'm trained in the gift and with the sword. No safer place than with me." He grinned, though it was clear he was more than a little suspicious of me.

"My camp is your camp, Commander," I acquiesced, and invited him to take the lone bedroll, the hospitality ingrained in me from the farm causing me to give up my bed for the night. Where would I sleep if he took me up on the offer?

"Please, I am not so lacking in chivalry to have a lady sleep on the ground." The commander whistled twice, the sound carrying on the wind as moonlight filled the camp. A horse of white trotted into view, its mane like freshly fallen snow. I gasped at the sight of her. Etienne perked up at her appearance too, head lifting from the grassy patch he had found to chew on.

Callum cooed to the beautiful horse till it pressed its head into his hands. He lifted a pack from the saddle and began to set up his own bed and tent.

I shivered from the wind whipping through my damp hair.

"What do I do now? He is staying here," I asked Shroding in my mind.

"I will keep watch while you sleep. Callum was an honorable man when I knew him. As long as I stay hidden, you should be safe."

"How do you know him?"

"He and I... grew up together. He was one of my only friends." He sighed with a heaviness that said far more than words could have. Something had happened between them, something Shroding was still wounded by, but was not ready to share with me just yet.

"I'll try to get some sleep, then," I agreed, and took my place on my bedroll.

"Would you like to rest in my tent?" Callum asked just as I closed my eyes.

I sat up abruptly. "I'm perfectly fine right here," I fumbled, completely losing my cool again.

"Haya, calm down, you are only making him more suspicious," Shroding warned.

"I thought you could only feel *my* emotions?" I snapped back, knowing my jumpy reactions were indeed making things worse.

"I don't need to feel his emotions to know he can sense how uncomfortable you are." He scoffed. "You're nervous, but it's not quite the same as before."

I flushed, taking in Callum's tight Krav suit, which without the adornments revealed a toned, corded body only won from years of training. I was not new to a man's strong physique—Micah, Theo and my dad were all well built from hard labor on the farm—but Callum was on a whole other level. His muscles had muscles, and they rippled and surged with every move he made. Just another thing about him that seemed to dance, and from the knowing tilt of his lips, he was well aware how gorgeous he was.

Callum bent at the edge of the hot spring and filled his canteen before speaking again.

"Your hair is damp. If you catch a chill, you will be sick for the first week of training at the garrison." He took a swig of water, not seeming fazed by how hot it was. "The tent will be warmer with two." Then he rose and sauntered across the boundary, kneeling next to my bedroll. Though the sword was still strapped to his side, something about him removing all the metal plates made him significantly more approachable and, to my dismay, terribly more attractive.

"Seriously, Haya, I know he is handsome, but you shouldn't let your guard down." Shroding's voice startled me.

"I don't mean to scare you," Callum offered, a hand coming to rest on my shoulder in a familiar way. With him so close I could see his eyes were lighter than the firelight had let on, though the color was still unclear to me; this too had me relaxing a little. Someone with such clear eyes could not mean me harm, right? "I promise you have nothing to fear from me tonight." He spoke with an assurance that was also comforting.

"Ever the charmer," Shroding seethed in my mind. "Haya, pull yourself together."

But I couldn't. Though I knew I should feel anxious, scared, all the things I had felt moments ago, the emotions were muted, muddled and getting farther and farther away. What was happening to me? I mean, he was devastatingly smooth, like honey butter over my mom's fresh-baked orange bread, but how was he doing this? I wasn't even the least bit afraid of him anymore.

"Strings, he is using his vibration gift. How could I have forgotten? He is an Orator, they can 'speak' to your emotions and manipulate them. Every emotion has a frequency, a vibration unique to it, and an Orator can tap into another person's emotional vibration and mess with the frequency, making them feel whatever the Orator wants. It is rare, like being a Healer, or a Wavemaster, who has both abilities."

"What is your nam—" Callum began.

"Commander." I choked on my words slightly. I might feel safe with Callum, but my mind was still mine, and I knew I should not trust him, especially if he was messing with my emotions. "I appreciate your offer, but I am quite warm by the fire."

He tilted his head. "I will not press you, but my tent is open should you change your mind."

"I won't."

"I feel like we got off on the wrong foot. My name is Commander McClain." He held out his arm to shake mine, a smirk lifting the corner of his mouth.

"As I said before, Commander." I shook his arm, out of respect, because my mother had raised me right, but I kept my face stern as I reminded him, "My business is my own."

"A girl barely of age traveling alone is unheard of. Not to mention the strength of the gift in you. You are asking for trouble, being alone in these woods. The Grieving have been sighted in these mountains." He held my arm as he spoke, and though I felt calm, his actions were raising red flags.

I lifted my chin. "I can handle myself. I am going to war, after all. The woods should not scare a warrior."

"Is that what you are?" His hand tightened on my arm as he hauled me onto my feet.

My heart pumped against my ribs, but I could not feel any fear. It was disorienting.

"Bold words for someone who has not yet started training. Tell me, have you learned Krav, how to move to the vibration dimension?" He pulled me in close and whispered. "Do you have a special gifting? A Healer, Orator or long-forgotten Wavemaster, perhaps?" He chuckled, but the sound was more like a puff of air than laughter. Was he mocking me? "Or is your strength because you have vibration sickness?" It seemed impossible, but his grip tightened, and I winced. "You want to become like the Grieving?"

Bile rose in my throat as I recalled the broken corpses of men who'd attacked the farmhouse, burning everything. He thought I was one of those monsters? My face scrunched in disgust.

"I would never become one of them," I spat, making it clear where I stood. Did he think I was the enemy? He'd invaded *my* camp, taking up the whole clearing with his high and mighty attitude, his demanding presence and hulking frame.

He scrutinized my face, satisfied with whatever he saw there. "I believe you, yet here you are, traveling alone, with a power in you greater than someone ten times your age."

"I don't know what you mean," I insisted, jaw tight. "I have yet to train," I reminded him, feigning ignorance. Why was he baiting me? Did he want me to lash out, to use the king's power? Had Shroding been wrong, did Callum know the power in me?

"Then shall we spar? I have been riding all day, and my muscles are tight. I could use the exercise." He let go of my arm, stepping back to stretch and showcase his point.

I looked away from his flexing biceps. "I don't even know the basic forms."

His grin was wicked with mischief as he crouched into a Krav stance. "Shall I teach you?"

———

"Place your foot here, fist loose, and move your thumb if you don't want to break it." Callum adjusted my stance for the millionth time. "Now glide through the flow I showed you." I did as I was told, enjoying the training more than I'd thought I would, though that could just be Callum's influence. Shroding had told me to agree to Callum's request, apparently recalling that Callum wasn't good at taking no for an answer. So here I was, learning basic forms from a rather pompous man and trying very hard and failing to not have fun.

We had not spoken much, other than to give and receive direction. When I finished the flow Callum had shown me, he smiled genuinely—or at least it seemed genuine, but I couldn't really trust my emotions with him around.

"Excellent, you are a fast learner. Now we can do some basic defensive training."

I made a noise akin to a laugh of despair. I was barely able to keep standing, I was so exhausted, the night finally catching up to me, and yet he wanted to teach me more? What was his angle? "Commander, I am very tired. Perhaps I should sleep, since I have to leave at first light as I said."

"Mhm." He rubbed his chin. "The first week of training is the worst," he agreed, seeming like he might acquiesce. "However, with your aptitude and vibration gift, I think you would be better suited for the academy in Erasmus or Romath. I can put in a special request for you to attend. You would get better training there than at the garrison."

I blinked. All this was to assess me and offer me an opportunity most people dreamed of? To have that kind of pull meant Callum was very high in rank, perhaps even above the title of commander as he claimed.

I shook my head. "I do not want recognition. Please allow me to go to the garrison as originally planned."

"You don't want to excel in your service to Shamar?"

I inhaled sharply. I was not my brother, and though he'd died doing what he thought was best for Shamar, I wanted to do what was best for Shroding, because in the end that would serve Shamar better. "I am just a farmer's daughter. I want to fight, survive and return home." The words would have been true if I had a home to return to.

Callum dropped into a fighting stance. "Very well." He extended his hand, waving me to come at him.

"Haya, this time he is trying to get you to use your gift."

"I figured as much," I thought back, holding my hands up in surrender. "Commander, I will lose to you."

"So you won't even try?"

"It would be poin—" I cut off as Callum unsheathed his sword and held the tip to the side of my throat. What a cheap move.

"You have an exceptional amount of power in you. Do not waste your potential, in desire for a normal life."

There was nothing normal about my life anymore. I was following a cat-prince through the mountains to turn him back into a man using the king's power inside me so he could kill Skithian, an evil entity who has plagued our world for thousands of years. But Callum was not to be trusted, so he could not know that. I needed to protect Shroding and the power inside me. The only way to do that was to either fight back or remove myself from the fight entirely. I didn't have the ability, even with the magnitude of the king's power, to win against Callum.

"Shroding, don't worry, I have a plan."

"Haya, I will not let him harm you."

"Trust me, and stay hidden," I assured him before closing my eyes and collapsing to the hard ground in my best swoon.

The blade nicked the side of my throat as I fell, the sting unpleasant, but not enough to have me open my eyes and give up the charade.

"Miss?" Callum questioned, his boots coming to rest at

my side. He lifted me in his arms, and I had to resist the urge to see what he was doing and demand he unhand me.

Strings, I hoped he bought the act.

"Haya, he is taking you into his tent. I can't see what is happening in there." Shroding sounded a bit panicked.

"I'll be fine." I assured him.

I heard the tent flap close, and what felt like fur brushed against my cheek as he laid me down.

"I underestimated how tired you might be," Callum muttered to himself, almost sounding regretful.

He touched the cut at my neck, and to hide my flinch, I rolled away, giving him my back, all the while begging in my mind for him to leave me be.

A weight fell over my shoulders. Had he put a blanket over me?

"Good night, farm girl. Rest while you can." Then he sighed, and after some movement I assumed he had settled down to sleep as well.

Good night, Commander, I thought as sleep did indeed take me, leaving my thoughts echoing with the faint rumble of Shroding's growl.

CHAPTER 6
A Dimension Deep

Pocket Dimension

I rolled to my side as the events of the last twenty-four hours flooded my mind. Confused as to where I was, I sat up frantically, looking for Shroding.

My pulse thrummed in my ears. I searched the clearing quickly. I was not in the tent anymore. The fire had gone out, and Etienne was not where I had left him. My breathing came in short bursts as panic welled within me. Then I looked, really looked, around. The world was hazy, unfocused.

Had I moved dimensions again while I slept? I covered my face with my hands, taking a few deep breaths. I needed to calm down.

"Prince?" I whispered tentatively.

The trees in the clearing rustled with the wind no louder than the puffs of breath leaving my lips. Cold settled around me. It was just like all the other times I'd been in the rip. The world began its descent into darkness. The clearing shifted from day to a blood-moon night. I swallowed thickly.

He'd promised to come. I waited a few more tremulous moments, sure the Wraiths would find me before he showed up.

Anxious, I shouted, "Prince Shroding, I need you to come right now!" I squeezed my eyes shut, letting my doubt rush over me, foolish as it was.

"Haya, I'm right here, don't doubt anymore." His gentle voice echoed in my mind as a presence settled in next to me. Scared to open my eyes, I shifted towards his voice and held out my shaking hands. His hands cupped mine, their warmth like sunrays on a winter day.

I gazed at him, and the darkness receded with his presence. Was I in the pocket with him now?

"Hello." He smiled, the smooth planes of his face crinkling to reveal a dimple on his left cheek. I tried to catch my breath as his dark brown eyes glittered with flecks of gold.

How could anyone look so perfect? Nothing about him was technically different from the last time we saw each other, and yet this meeting was totally different. I was different. A closeness was between us now, because without knowing who he really was, I had opened up to him, shared my thoughts with him, spilled my tears figuratively and literally over him. And he'd taken it all with a patience and kindness I was so grateful for.

Looking back there were a lot of things for me to be mortified and ashamed about, but he did not seem to mind my failures on the farm. If I had only been able to see who he really was sooner, maybe the farm wouldn't have fallen to ash and ruin; so many lives devastated. But that was my shame to bear, and now with him before me again in human form, I could only think of the good we would be able to do for Shamar. Just as I had said to Micah, I intended to do whatever was best for Shroding, because he really would be the one to save us all.

His dark hair fell in waves around his angular face. Reaching up and I tucked the strands behind his ear, my fingers tracing over the shell. Ears and hair I had touched without a second thought when he was Iri. Things I shouldn't do now that he was a prince; my future king. Affection I needed not to show.

Yet, I found myself wondering if it would be okay. If I saved him, would it be okay to be this close? If I helped him, could I mean something more to him? I didn't know what saving Shroding would mean. What more would it cost me? More loss, more pain? Maybe even my life? But would my death matter to someone so important? Could I become someone important to him? Even without the king's power? I knew I shouldn't, but I wanted to become someone he couldn't live without.

He did not shy away from my touch. He simply waited, his eyes not leaving mine as he watched me take him in again as a man.

"I have a lot of questions." I sighed, my brows pinching, my hand falling to rest in my lap.

"So you have said." He chuckled. "Let's not ignore the obvious."

For a moment I had no idea what he meant. Was he referring to all the thoughts I had just had? Strings, I'd forgotten he was probably listening to everything.

When I said nothing, my face warming in embarrassment, he offered, "Callum?" Then he crossed his arms, giving me a chiding look.

I exhaled my relief. He was referring to Commander Callum McClain? Of course he was.

"Are you sure fainting was the best way out of that situation?" He pinned me with a look that had heat returning to my neck. "Or were you just looking for a way to get into his arms?" I would have fancied him jealous if not for the teasing glint in his eyes.

I lifted my chin. "I don't know what you're talking about."

"Your face was completely red." Shroding deadpanned.

"It was warm from the fire," I insisted.

"Of course it was. You do realize those in the king's court are all very attractive, right? You will need to get used to seeing handsome ladies and men if you plan to travel with me once I am human again."

Despite my earlier wishes to become someone he needed and wanted with him always, my next words teased just the opposite. "What makes you think I would want to travel with you after I help you? You will have to go to war, after all, and I'm not sure I'm cut out for that. Maybe I'll go back to the farm and rebuild when this is all done." I shrugged, but he had to know those words held zero truth to them. I did not think returning was something I could ever do, but truthfully I could not think that far in advance anyway. Still, I did want to stay with him. So if he meant what he said and asked me to stick around after, I would, in a heartbeat.

But for now the only thing that mattered was making Shroding a human again, and I still had no idea how to do that.

He was silent for a long time, my lack of tact in flirting clearly killing the mood. "As much as I hate to admit it, it was good Callum taught you a few basic Krav forms."

Taking the out, I nodded. "I do need to get used to the gift if I'm going to use it to help you." I crossed my legs, sitting in front of him. "So what's the deal with you and Callum?"

"Let's just say not all friends from my past can be trusted; I'm just not sure which ones can and can't. That just means you will need to learn to fight sooner than later. Because, unfortunately for you, wild animals are not the only thing you have to fear. The Wraiths will never give up, and before this is over, you will face the Grieving again. So all good humor aside, I think it would be best for you to get some training. I can teach you all I know when we are together here."

"I will learn whatever I need to in order to help you," I promised.

He stood up, brushing off his pants, then folded his hands behind his back in a proper way that screamed he had been raised as royalty. He lifted his chin, looking down at me.

"Wait, you mean like right now?" I asked, leaning forward where I sat.

He raised an eyebrow. "It won't be anything too difficult." He smirked. "Promise."

I had settled down on a rock next to the cave opening, while Shroding paced back and forth, shoulders back as he taught.

"To gain control of and strengthen your gift, it takes more than just linear skill development. The strength of the gift is measurable in two ways. First is by skill. If one trains in the art of Krav, then they are able to use their gift with greater force than someone who has not trained. Second is focus or concentration. Through utilizing the control developed during Krav in conjunction with meditation, one can deepen their gift."

"Okay...?"

"Imagine a lake," he advised gently. I did. "If one does not have the gift, they will never be able to touch the water. But if they do have the gift, they can. When one's skill in Krav is not trained, that person can only go into the lake up to their ankles, but as they learn Krav and develop, they can go out further, to their knees, hips, and head. Eventually, after training in meditation, they can go under the surface. Imagine the lake is deep and endless. Once you go under, you are only as strong as the depth you can go, with the breath you can hold."

"Okay..." I said again, understanding this was what he meant when he said it was not linear. After one goes under, it is no longer horizontal growth but vertical.

"Most people never get very deep because their body can't withstand the pressure of the metaphorical water. Hence why the enemy found a way around the physical barriers by using the gift on themselves. The sickness allows them to go deeper under the lake, but at the cost of their physical body. They die because of it."

"Does the lake have a bottom?"

"Only the king can swim the deepest, only his body can withstand the pressure. It isn't known if there is a bottom."

"What about the Seraphs, or those with special giftings? They are stronger than normal people with the gift."

"Yes, there are those who are different. They are different in that they don't go into the water, they pull the water up and around them. Skill is a part of it, but the bigger part is they have been given a unique gift from the Creator of Strings. Seraphs moved through time and space, but the cost for them was their lives. For each new world they explored, they lost years of life. The more they explored, the faster they would die."

"That's so sad."

"Everything has a price. Everything," he said grimly. Did he know the price saving him would end up costing me? "Still, they got to see things no one else would ever see, not even the king."

"And the other giftings, what are their costs?"

"The Wavemasters were given tremendous range for their vibration ability; this range was only as good as their ability to concentrate. They could use their gift from miles away, finding a person simply by listening for their distinct sound, but only by spending hours of the day in meditation. They lived half their lives in the vibration dimension, memorizing and learning all forms of color and sound. Seeing and hearing the vibrations all around them. So they can understand how to find people and change emotions much like Orators do. Most go mad, and those who don't, struggle to relate to people in this dimension. That is their cost."

I wanted to ask about Healers, but something Shroding said made me have another more pressing question. "If Krav comes before meditation, won't there be a problem for me since I don't know Krav, but I have been moving dimensions and training in going to the vibration dimension? Isn't that like diving into the deep end before learning to swim in the shallows?"

"Keeping with the analogy, yes."

"Is that bad?"

He ran his fingers through his hair. "There is an order to things, yes. So technically it could very well become an issue."

"What kind of issue?"

"The power could turn on you, like vibration sickness but by accident. Or if you spend too much time in the vibration world before you are ready, you could go blind in the real world. It was not uncommon for that to happen to Wavemasters in training."

"What!"

"But the king's power is different. It is capable of far more than even I understand. If there were going to be side effects, we would have started to see them already."

I wasn't comforted, but still, I didn't have much of a choice. I had to get better at using the gift so I could help Shroding. Everything has a cost, and I supposed it was a risk I would have to take. "I didn't think the power could hurt me." I looked down at my hands with apprehension.

"No one ever thinks having power will hurt them, until they have been hurt by it." He spoke with a firmness that said he very much lived out that truth himself.

"So, maybe to be safe, we practice some more Krav, build on what Callum showed me?" I suggested.

"My thoughts precisely," he said with a dangerous edge to his voice, and held out a hand to me.

CHAPTER 7
Beacon To Me

I slipped my hand into his, doing my best to ignore how large and firm it was. My hand all but disappeared in his. I followed him to the side of the cave. The pocket dimension was bright though the sun was not visible. Everything else looked much the same, but where I expected the air to feel cold, it was comfortable. Neither the chill of the mountains nor the burn of heat filled the air; it was just perfect. Though strange, it was welcome. At least while I slept I did not feel cold.

"First things first. Krav basic forms." He let go of my hand and turned to stand in front of me. "Core is everything," he advised, knees bending and arms tucking in. "Hold your hands here and here, feet no more than two lengths apart, staggered."

I copied his stance, finding it similar to the stance Callum had shown me.

We did this a few times, Shroding showing a stance and me following suit. After he ran through the forms Callum had shown me, he added new ones. Each new move built upon the last. Each bend, twist and kick repetitive and yet slightly different.

"Square your hips." He reached out, so focused on teaching me that he didn't realize his thumbs were pressing into the tender space between my hip bone and belly. I swallowed noisily as he slowly pivoted my hips to the front then side. "Shift like this when you transition to the next stance," he guided me.

"R-Right." I practiced again, dropping into the next form. He stepped back, holding his chin, watching carefully.

"That was better." He nodded, crossing his arms, satisfied.

Heat was crawling up my neck, and I knew any second my thoughts would betray me. I needed a distraction.

"So," I began, continuing to move between forms. "Where will you go after you become human again?" I prompted, a nervous bubble forming in my chest. Would he stay at Palace Moreh in Tyndale or go to Castle Judahall in Romath? Could we still be together when this was over?

"I will go where the court needs me most," he answered simply, then hesitated, running his hand through his hair. "Do you think you will go back to Wycliff when this is all over?"

I shrugged noncommittally. "I don't think there's anything to go back to."

"What about your mom?"

"The farm is gone, and she wasn't from Wycliff originally; she only stayed because of my father."

His brows knit. "Where is she from?"

"Romath, actually." I lifted my arm into the next form, remembering to breathe evenly. "So I suppose when we reunite, we may go to the capital. I've never been. Maybe the change of scenery will be good for us." I rotated, turning so my back was to him, not liking how we were already talking about life apart. I hadn't meant for the conversation to go this way.

When I ended the flow, I tilted my head to look at him over my shoulder.

His lips were pursed in thought. "Most likely... I will end up in Romath as well."

And just like that, I was hoping, perhaps foolishly, to stay by his side. Would he let me? Would staying by his side mean the Wraiths would continue to come after me? That I would have to go to war? Could I endanger my life by choice, knowing I was all my mother had left? But wasn't I already doing that now?

He interrupted my thoughts. "None of this will be easy. Are you sure you don't want to go back?" he asked, as if my teasing from earlier had actually concerned him, as if he needed reassurance.

I twisted in the stance he'd just taught me and gave a playful punch to his arm, trying to lighten the mood. "I would think following you into these mountains, riding off, away from everything I've ever known, would have proven my commitment."

He rubbed his arm wearily, and though one corner of his mouth lifted, he still looked sad as he said, "People have left me for far less." He dropped his head. Was he referring to Callum, to his other friends? "My presence in your life has only brought pain and destruction for you, so I would not fault you if you chose to go back." He sighed, kneeling next to the embers, poking the charred wood with a stick.

I put my hand on his shoulder and knelt beside him, seeing the thirteen-year-old who'd lived a half life in the shadows with only three friends for company. The boy who'd given up his whole life for the sake of the kingdom, for everyone. He may have grown into the body of a man, but his heart was still as fragile as the boy.

"Listen." Lifting my hand to his cheek, I turned his face to look at me. "I'm not going anywhere. Wherever you go, I will go. If you want me to stay, I will stay."

"Haya..." He breathed my name like a caress, taking my hand from his cheek to brush his lips over my knuckles. "You have no idea..." He flexed the fingers of his other hand over his knee. "I waited..." He looked up, our gazes locking. Heat pooled under my skin, and this time I had no fire to blame it on, so I tried to hide my disquiet with a laugh.

"Waited?" I choked, trying very hard not to look at the gentle slope of his lips lingering inches from my skin. The way the world had shattered and come together, tiny fragments of my soul finding a rhythm, a new life, when those lips had touched mine. Our kiss from so long ago had filled me with a strange hunger, one I did not want to dwell too hard on. I took a deep breath, trying to relax the tension in my body.

His dark eyes searched mine, the corner of his mouth lifting as he leaned in, his face dangerously close. If the wind blew just a little harder, I would have fallen over, and if he had tried to know my thoughts at that moment, all he would have heard was a string of incoherent dribble.

Unable to resist any longer, I dropped my gaze to his lips, and we both inhaled. Our breaths mingled as his mouth dipped to mine.

The pull to kiss him, to reach up and taste him again was as implicit as the need to touch him when the moonlight poured over his fur. The same insatiable need to get close rocketed through me, a sound like a whimper escaping my lips. A cursed noise that had Shroding halting and withdrawing, His hand let go of mine as he sat back, blinking, perplexed. He *looked unsure of what he'd just been about to do. As if he too had been beckoned by that undeniable pull, except he had been able to deny it.*

"That was..." He blew out a breath.

"You felt it too? The pull?" I sank back on my heels, feeling like a chasm had opened between us.

He nodded evenly. "Even before that day on the dandelion hill. It's been like a beacon, calling to me."

My brow furrowed. He was pulled to me before he met me? Was it because the power called to him, wanting to be reunited with him?

"So when the power manifested in me, you sensed it somehow?"

Shroding put his face in his hands and laughed. For a moment I was startled. He looked at me with the most desperately forlorn expression. His eyes glistened in the corners. "Felt it, sure, I saw it too. It was like nothing I had ever seen. When I say beacon, I mean you were a literal beacon—streams of purple light filled the sky." He looked up at the clouds, hands falling into his lap. "I only knew the streams of light were calling me because I can't see in color... but I could see them. Once I became a cat, I lost the ability to see color in this dimension and in the real world." He closed his eyes. "Still, those purple lights shimmered in the sky like moonlight on water. At first I thought something was terribly wrong." He chuckled. "Then I knew because I could see the color that they were for me. A sign of something important. The only color I had seen in two hundred years, and I ran straight for them." His dark gaze met mine. "Straight to you."

I didn't want to, but I blushed. My whole body flushed like it had when I ran laps around the fields as a kid. I shifted in my seat.

"That was the day on the dandelion hill? You appeared out of nowhere." I remembered that day now in a new light. The way my hands had looked see-through, the intense gaze of the beautiful cat. The way he'd purred louder as I approached.

"I had watched you all day from the tree line. I had planned to approach you, but you came to me first. You walked right up the hill and sat down. When I saw your hand vibrate..." He took a deep, shaking breath and opened his eyes. "I never felt anything like it. Describing it wouldn't do it justice."

I blushed harder, glad he couldn't see in color. "Try?" I coaxed, my curiosity getting the better of me.

He stared down at his open palms. "I suppose it's like when you have two magnets attracting each other, but you hold them just the slightest bit apart. That tension. Like there is something physically between them, drawing them together. That is what it was like, or at least the closest thing I can describe it to."

"I think I kind of get what you mean," I reasoned. If it had been anything like the kiss, then I understood the something in between. Could that something be felt in both dimensions? I had felt it here in this world, and he was telling me he felt it in the real world while he was a cat. Did he feel that something here with me now?

Without even touching, I was hyperaware of every movement, every breath he made. We were silent for a long time, both unsure what to make of the connection between us. Most of all I wondered if the connection was all I felt.

When he said nothing and the awkwardness grew too heavy, I got to my feet and continued Krav, moving through the flow with focus and intention. After a while he took the cue, and we continued training, but it wasn't long before he broke the silence.

"Things might not have happened the way either of us wanted, but they happened the way they needed to. I can't fathom your loss, and I know you worry still about your mother, but please know I am glad it is you. I'm glad the power led me to you."

I shook my head. "I'm not so sure. I have done nothing for you except fight you this whole time, doubting, questioning and fearing what's to come."

"You have every right to, this is not something you have a guidebook on how to handle. Neither of us really know how this is going to unfold. Still..." He reached out, stopping my flow and turning me to face him. "Haya, I trust you. I have trusted you since the beginning. I couldn't risk you running away. Not when I could see you in so much pain every night. Fighting for your life. I had to let you find the truth for yourself."

His honesty opened a floodgate in me, and everything I had tried to shut in, keep tucked away, rose up. "All I wanted was for my family to come home. Now I don't know what I want. I had thought I knew myself, my life, but those things are all gone."

He squeezed my shoulders, taking me into his arms. I had not realized I was crying till I saw the wetness on his shirt. He patted my back and whispered over and over again. "It's going to be okay." Even though I knew they wouldn't come back, that I couldn't rewind the time, that his words shouldn't have been comforting, they were. I clung to those soft words of hope. It was going to be okay. I was going to be okay, and despite feeling like a boat with no anchor, I believed him.

If I was going to be brave enough to fight the Grieving and

Wraiths, I would need to be more than just physically strong. I would have to be mentally fortified. Facing the ugly, monstrous anguish inside me was only the start. I knew what I must do. So I did. I thought through the losses and let myself feel each one. Let the sobs expunge the last of my energy and heaviness till I was empty, hollowed out. Till there was enough room in me to be filled by something new.

"I will help you till the end," I mumbled through the tears. I may not know if I would see my friends or mom again, but right now, in this moment, I knew where I was needed most. That would have to be enough for me.

My father and mother, Theo, and Micah, all loved me and believed in me. With them out of my reach now, I was left to believe in myself. So that was what I would do. I would not be helpless, but believe in my ability, the king's power—this new purpose.

CHAPTER 8

Escape

"Haya, come on." Shroding's voice filled my mind while a persistent push of fur brushed my neck.

I waved the fur away, eyes popping open when I realized it was Shroding's face.

"Sorry." I sat up and scanned the tent. We were alone. Where had Callum gone?

"He is chasing down his horse. I spooked her so you and I could get away."

Shroding bounded out of the tent and stopped next to Etienne. I followed after him. "Quickly pack what you can, he won't be gone long, what with that whistle skill." And just as he said it, the melody carried over the wind.

"Why didn't he just whistle from camp like he did last night?" I wondered, shaking off the haze of sleep and grabbing my bedroll, pack and canteen.

"I might have made it a bit difficult for the horse to come to him," Shroding answered with a glint of humor in his eyes.

Curious, I raised my eyebrows but didn't question it.

Coming around the side of the tent, I tripped over Callum's pack, and an apple rolled out. My stomach growled at the sight. He'd either left in a hurry or was more trusting than he ought to be.

"Or I put it there to take with us." Shroding answered my thoughts.

"Are you sure? I almost feel bad for him," I muttered, grabbing his pack with the rest of my supplies and strapping everything over the saddle. I wasn't one to steal normally, but my situation was not normal, so the Creator would just have to forgive this one.

"Callum is your superior. Let's think of it as him providing for his subordinate," Shroding offered, a childlike mischief to his tone that made me wonder if he really thought of Callum as an enemy. His antics were more like a friend playing a prank on a close confidant than someone trying to escape a villain.

Shroding leapt into the trees, and I hoisted myself up onto Etienne to trail after him.

A wall of clouds ferried in with the sun, casting the sky in a ominous gray, making it hard to tell the time. Though my sweater was thick, it would not keep me warm through the snow-laden nights ahead, the deeper we went into the mountains. When we were a good distance from the camp I asked, "Will he follow?"

"Callum is not one to give up. He is no doubt tracking us. But not for long. We can lose him in the coming storm."

———

Wolves howled in the distance, making the night more eerie

than I was comfortable with. A deep chill traveled down my spine.

After our escape we both settled into a thoughtful silence. The winds and sputtering rain made navigating the trail treacherous, and our attention focused on simply moving ahead.

I opened Callum's pack, finding packages of wrapped food, to my delight, but I stopped searching when my hand closed over a brush. Pulling it out, I kissed it and proceeded to comb through my wild tresses, not caring that with each stroke my hair crunched like the hay it was so similar in color to.

"Look!" I said joyfully, holding out the comb for Shroding to see. It was surprisingly feminine-looking, with pink and yellow gems along the neck. Had Shroding known there would be a brush in Callum's pack?

Shroding chuckled knowingly. "Callum was always a bit vain about his hair. So I figured there was a good chance one might be stashed inside."

My insides warmed at Shroding's devious yet thoughtful scheme.

Though Shroding said the comb was Callum's, it appeared too elegant of an instrument for such a gruff soldier. Two initials curled at the base of the neck. *N.M.* Could it belonged to a girlfriend, or wife? Might it be sentimental? I frowned, hoping it was not something he would miss. Perhaps I should not have taken his bag so recklessly, even if the food would sustain me for the duration of our travel, barring no detours.

Brushing the thoughts aside—nothing could be done about it now—I braided and tied my hair back with a cord from my pack. Hair saved and my mood lifted, I practiced with the gift, moving through to the vibration dimension, feeling out with the gift as Shroding had taught me. A pricking sensation began in my fingers, warming and spreading through my arms as I accessed the power.

Eyes closed, I focused on my breath, letting the blackness behind my eyes settle around me till I was sitting in a world of darkness. In this unseen world, the colors of each living thing's vibration sprang to life. At first it was like little sparks, then they grew into strings that glowed a myriad of colors. I could almost make out the shapes of the nature around me, wrapping and twisting around each other like music bars. The outline of trees and mountains shimmered with the growing vibrations. Every tree had its own vibration, the hum like a song. It was amazing. I turned my head, seeing behind closed eyes a world I hadn't known existed before Shroding taught me how to find it. I could see the outline of animals in the distance, each glowing a vivid color. Each humming a unique melody.

Still, the loudest sound I could hear was my breathing. In and out. Until my head turned to see Shroding's form. He wasn't a cat but a man wrapped in bronze and gold. The colors that twisted around him reached out, connecting to the other living colors around him. When the bronzed gold touched another colorful vibration, it would glow brighter, its hum louder. Like how Shroding's purr intensified at my touch. It was as if he was giving extra life to the vibrations around him. The hum of everything else was a hodgepodge of sounds compared to the clear song vibrating off him. I realized I had stopped breathing when the colors and sounds suddenly vanished and the world went dark once more.

"Haya!"

I had gotten so caught up in the song and colors of the world, I hadn't realized I had started to slip from the saddle.

Shroding had broken through the haze of my mind at the last second, before I completely tumbled off.

I opened my eyes, gasping as if I had been underwater. I righted myself on the saddle, and the tingling in my fingers vanished.

"Did you see it?" he asked, moving to walk alongside Etienne.

I nodded, remembering the energy of everything around me. The song he had given off. "You are beautiful," I whispered.

His tail twitched and lifted. "My father used to say that. He used to say seeing my vibrations helped him understand himself."

"How is that?"

"Ours were the same. He couldn't see his own. No one can see their own vibration, the sound or color. You can only see outside yourself."

I hadn't tried to see myself, so I nodded.

"Instead of seeing yourself, you can feel your vibration," he continued.

"Feel it?" I asked, my brow furrowed.

"Yes. For everyone it feels different. Did you feel yours?"

I glanced at my hands. "I think so..." I recalled the pinpricks on my fingers. "What is yours like?"

"When I had the gift, I felt it in my mouth first, like fire on my tongue. When I swallowed, it filled my whole body."

The crease in my brow deepened. "That sounds painful."

"It's not." He laughed. "What was yours like?"

"Like getting pricked by needles in my hands."

"And that doesn't sound painful?" he joked.

"It turned warm and spread up my arms, but it stopped there, I got distracted."

"You did amazingly. Most people don't even see the vibrations this early on in training."

"Really?!"

"The king's power will make it easy for you. You will probably excel faster than most."

"I see..." I sighed, feeling a little cheated, like my effort was of little consequence.

"Well, the king's power wants to be used. Its purpose is to bring balance. It wouldn't be helpful for anyone if it was hard to maneuver. But don't let that confuse you—it is more powerful than a regular gift, and it takes tremendous will and concentration to use. You did great," he emphasized.

"That makes sense." I agreed a little more validated. "I'll keep practicing."

"Good, but maybe not while on horseback?" he suggested.

I stuck to the arm movements Callum had taught me, keeping my eyes open and alert, which seemed to put Shroding at ease, even though he continued to look back at me from time to time to assess my stability in the saddle.

Hours passed in silence as we journeyed deeper into the mountains.

Shroding began to favor one side over another. Were his paws hurting him?

I twisted the ends of my hair.

"Something wrong?" Shroding asked, turning around. I couldn't see his eyes. The sun was setting, and the light behind him put his face in shadow.

He had been leading the way, running the whole time just to keep ahead of Etienne's long strides.

"Are you tired? Do you want to sit up here with me?" I offered, patting the spot in front of the saddle.

"No, no, I'm not tired at all."

"Are you sure? We have been going for hours, it's gonna get dark soon." I looked up to see the topaz sun kiss the tops of the vast western mountain range.

"It's best for me to keep leading the way from here," he insisted, running a bit farther ahead.

I understood him not wanting people to pick him up as a cat, that could be a bit demeaning.

"If we are going to sleep outside again, I will need a coat or blanket or something." The higher into the mountains we climbed, the colder the nights would become. The rain would probably turn to snow at some point. "It does no one any good if I die of hypothermia," I added with a weak laugh.

"Oh." He paused pensively. "I didn't anticipate this," he said softly, and it seemed he had not intended for me to hear that.

I forced a smile, looking up at the clouds that drizzled, and let out a hollow laugh. "Good thing it's not too bad tonight, I think I will be fine." I stretched lazily, my arms high overhead, and yawned.

His gaze shifted to the trees, a look of concentration in his reflective eyes. "There is a small shed that way. We can camp there for tonight."

I squinted through the foliage. "I don't see anything."

He chuckled, the sound genuine if not a bit smug. "You're not a cat."

"Fair point." I smiled and followed him.

We continued till we came to the small shed abandoned in the woods. It looked like it might have been used as a hunting shed at some point. Perhaps we were near a town after all.

The door was moss-covered and the hinges so rusted I had to grunt a little to open it. I shuffled into the small space.

The stone walls were crumbling. The one opposite me was almost completely knocked out, exposing the room to the elements. A pile of straw was pushed into one corner. The floorboards were nonexistent, as dirt and moss had overpowered the small space.

"I guess I found my bed for the night."

I tossed the bedroll down beside the straw, as it would help keep me insulated. Shroding came in, eyeing the ceiling, which had a rather large hole.

"If it rains harder, this won't do much for cover," he said regretfully.

I sat down, also looking up at the hole in the ceiling, which was big enough for two people to fit through. At least it would allow the smoke from a fire to exit the small shed.

Shroding's silver fur transitioned to a soft amethyst as a sliver of moonlight broke through the clouds and streamed in through the moss-covered opening.

I watched in rapture once more. The strong pull to be close to him was almost tangible. He came up next to the bedroll.

Reflexively I threaded my fingers through his fur. He flinched a little and then relaxed, and I wondered if this was offensive to him. I had pet him so often when he was just Iri, but he wasn't just Iri anymore. "Does this bother you?" Something I should have asked before, when I caressed his hair in the pocket dimension.

A flock of birds flew overhead, almost drowning out his soft reply.

"No," he whispered, his tone remorseful, as if he wished it did.

His purring grew louder, and I smiled.

I knew well enough, from the stray cats on the farm, that cats purr happily when pet just the right way, yet Shroding was always purring when I was with him. "Why do you always purr?" I asked.

He didn't say anything for a long moment, and my cheeks heated. Had I said something foolish? Was he mad? Being a cat was probably hard enough without me probing with silly questions.

Timidly I poked his side, desperate for him to alleviate the nervous butterflies in my chest.

"Sorry I was... trying to think of how to explain it. It's kind of embarrassing." He sighed. "Honestly I had hoped you wouldn't notice."

Relieved I hadn't offended him, I poked his side again. "It just means you like me, right?" I teased.

"Well, not exactly." I deflated a little at his serious tone. "It's because you have the king's power. It's like we are on the same frequency, if that makes sense." It didn't, so I shook my head, and he tried again. "Let's say we have two objects that both vibrate at the same frequency." I nodded slightly. "So the sound produced by object A, you, causes Object B, me, to vibrate."

"Oh?"

"It's not as extreme as in other cases of this phenomenon. Basically you cause me to purr. It was another reason I knew you were different."

"You mean besides being able to feel my emotions?" I teased.

His ears twitched. "I had plenty of reasons to notice you."

The idea of him noticing anything about me made my foolish heart skip. I wanted to ask for more details, but he playfully nipped at my hand laced into the fur at his side.

"We should get a fire going." He slipped outside, putting an end to the conversation.

Though all I wanted to do was lie down and eat the food from Callum's pack, I figured it was prudent to try to fill in at least one of the holes in the shed. My unfrostbitten body would thank me later. So while Shroding disappeared into the trees to find firewood, I scavenged for any large rocks or fallen branches I could pile up against the outside of the broken wall.

The moments alone in the trees released a torrent of emotions I had been doing my best to hide from. Cold and hungry, I found myself longing for my mom. For her comfort and dependability. For her to come alongside me and tell me everything was going to be okay.

I shoved a large branch into place against the wall.

Where was she now, what was she doing? Had she seen the farm? Had Micah passed on my message? Had the soldiers at the Citadel reached Erasmus yet?

I shoved another branch into place, surprised when my knees buckled. I leaned into the stones, waiting for my vision to steady. Tears pricked my eyes as a wave of panic gripped me.

The air turned thick and damp. The way it coated my throat and left a film over the skin beneath my clothes told me the storm had finally reached us. Like the torrent of emotions had broken free in me, so did the rain from the sky.

My whole life was gone, and now I was on a journey to do something I did not fully understand. In the last few weeks everything I identified with, everything that had made me... *me*... had been slowly ripped out of my hands till my hands were left shaking, vacant of all I used to clutch vigorously in them.

What was I supposed to do with that? I was spiraling, I knew the signs—and just when I'd thought I was accepting things. The more I thought about my family, Micah, the more I wanted to shut everything out. As much as I wanted to open up to Shroding, I knew if we started we would end up talking about all the things I wasn't sure I was ready to share. About Father and Theo, about all the pain. How it hurt so much I couldn't breathe. As if talking about the loss would make it feel. Like sharing my most precious memories would lessen their worth somehow. As if holding the memories in, keeping them close—secret—gave me control over their power to break me, when in fact it only fueled their ability to rip me apart.

With deliberate slowness I made my way around the shed and through the creaking door, my body soaked from the onslaught of rain.

In the moments I had been trying to hold myself together, Shroding had not only built a fire but had covered up half the hole in the ceiling, leaving only enough room for the smoke to filter out.

"Haya?"

I slumped against the inside wall, turning my face to hide the fresh tears. "Shroding." I whispered absently, picking at the moss between the stones as I pressed my cheek into the cool, rough surface. "I know I asked for the truth," I began, "and I followed you without knowing where we were going. Without knowing what I would really have to do. I mean, I could be certifiably insane at this point... following a strange cat who turned out to be a prince. I know you tried your best to explain, and I get it, I really do, I just… I just feel like my head is going to explode. I don't know how to process, how to… to…" I choked on the anxiety clawing to get into every part of my soul.

I shivered, feeling the difference between the front of my wet clothes, warmed by the fire, and my back.

"You're cold," Shroding said, walking past the fire to me.

"It's fine," I lied.

He pulled the mat a little closer to the fresh flames and nudged my arm till I crawled over to the bedroll. He found food in the pack and carried it to me. "Everything is a bit more bearable when you are warm and fed," he encouraged.

I ate the packaged food, letting the heat of the fire burn away my gooseflesh.

"I should have thought this through a bit more. It's been so long since I've been human…" He trailed off, and I could tell he was upset that I was uncomfortable, but nothing could really be done about it anyway. He had thick winter fur to protect himself from the elements. It wasn't like he could take it off and share it, though I did not doubt he would if it were possible.

I smiled and lay down as if to say, "See, I'm fine, snug as a bug in a rug."

He looked at me perplexed; he must have heard my thoughts. "This phrase… Is it a good thing to be a bug in a rug?"

I snorted, having forgotten that some language is lost on the poor prince. "Yes, it is. You can be one too." I pat the place next to me.

His shadow passed over me, and his furry face leaned down, our noses almost touching. "If it's okay, I will lie here," he said, curling his body around the top of my head. He was warm, and I could feel his breathing. My heart fluttered at his kindness.

"Oh, um, sure," I stammered. It did feel warmer having him insulate my head. My mom had always said heat escapes the body most from the head and back. "When should we get moving?" I sighed, closing my eyes. The faint purring in his chest and the soft whistling of his inhales and exhales mixed in an almost musical rhythm.

"It's best for us to wait till the rain stops," he assured me, but I could tell there was more he wanted to say.

Slowly, as if guided by loving arms, I curled up on the bedroll, the thrum of Shroding's purr and the crackle of the fire together creating a song of deep sleep I could do nothing but succumb to.

CHAPTER 9
From Your Lips

POCKET DIMENSION

I sat up, knowing I was in the rip. The shed was the same, the space small and cold, and the darkness of the Wraiths was brewing around me. I fought off the panic, took a deep breath and called, "Prince Shroding." Within a moment he appeared in front of me, and the whole dimension lit up in his presence.

He lounged across the pile of straw stacked in the corner, one knee bent, his arms crossed behind his head against the wall.

"Hello." He greeted me, his smile self-assured and almost a little coy.

"Hi," I squeaked, mortified by how a simple smile could make my voice all high and breathy.

He raised a brow, giving me a measured look that had me longing to crawl under a rock.

Not even a minute in, and I was embarrassing myself. Why was it so hard talking to him when he was a human?

When he was just Iri I let my words flow freely, letting him be my confidant. Would I be able to do that as readily with him again someday? Or would his human form always leave me tongue-tied?

It wasn't just me who sensed the shift between us. I was sure he had too. The change was almost imperceptible, but there. I was definitely more self-conscious around him. When he was just in my imagination, I had indulged in his good looks, but now, after really talking to him, it was wrong to relegate him down to just a devastatingly handsome prince—which he still was, but he also was a person. A real, capricious, intelligent person with a history and a story still unfolding. An almost flesh and blood prince who I was trying very hard not to think about kissing again.

My eyes had found focus on the soft curve of his lips, so I quickly banished that thought and averted my gaze.

"Why do you do that?"

My stomach dropped. What did he mean? Why did I look lustfully at his mouth? Or was he asking why I looked away? Had he wanted me to keep looking? Blood drained from my face as I met his eyes.

"W-What do you mean?"

"Why do you call me Prince Shroding?" He tilted his head, smile gone as he watched me.

"You are the prince." I swallowed.

He sat up, feet on the ground, and leaned forward, forearms on his knees. "I was your pet cat. My title should not change that."

I blinked. "So you want me to call you Iri?"

His eyes flashed. "Shroding is fine."

I blinked again. Was he wanting me to speak to him informally? As a friend, not as a subject? Was he teasing me, or pointing out how rude I had been, before I knew he was the future king? "I'm so sorry for the way I treated you before. As you know, I had no clue who you were."

His brows knit. "Strings, I feel all sorts of emotions from you, but not a single one makes sense to me." He leaned in till his hands rested on my shoulders, one knee on the ground. "I'm asking you to call me Shroding. Just Shroding. I don't want you to treat me any differently now that you know who I am. I suppose I should have made that more clear a while ago."

"Shroding." I breathed each letter of his name, testing each sound as they left my lips, realizing I had not spoken his name aloud, without the title, since the moment after we kissed.

Did he realize that too?

His dark eyes dropped to my lips, and all the air vanished from the small shed with that one look.

With wide eyes I watched him lean closer. Tension roared between us.

"Is it really okay?" I whispered, my question asking far more than he was probably aware. Was it okay to have kissed him before, could I again? Was it okay to want him? Was there a possible future where we could be an us?

Either he was choosing to be ignorant or he really had no idea about the tangle of longing I had for him, because he smiled, pat me on the shoulder and said, "Of course it is. So I better not hear the word prince come from your lips again." It was only when he winked that I became certain he knew exactly what he was doing.

By the Strings, he was trouble.

His grin turned knowing. "My sincerest apologies for troubling you." Slowly he brushed my hair over my shoulder, fingers feather-light across the side of my neck. "What's troubling you most about me?"

He was teasing me, toying with me. There was no way he was oblivious to the upheaval of emotions he was stirring in me. Still, why was he doing this? For fun, practice, curiosity, or some other reason?

"Right, well, um." That! That! I wanted to yell, that is trouble. All of him. Everything. His handsome four-hundred-year-old prince self was enough trouble to take down the most confident of girls. I didn't stand a chance. "You, um—" I coughed, my brain stuttering.

Iri, he's just Iri. Just an annoyingly watchful cat. Strings, if only that were true. But the thought of Iri had me calming down a bit.

"I'm deeply troubled by how you will adjust to being human again." I grinned, proud of the way I sashayed around his too tempting question. "Won't you miss being a cat?" I hedged.

He watched me for a beat. Then, shrugging, he sat back on the straw. "I've been one for half my life, I'm sure I will miss it. It has its pros."

"Like what?" I asked, intrigued.

"Cat naps, for sure. Night vision and impeccable hearing. Then there is not needing as much food. Oh, and running is totally different too, you run with your whole body. That split second where all four paws are off the ground..." He sighed wistfully. "Unreal. What I imagine flying might feel like." He looked at his fingernails innocently. "Oh, the flexibility is fun too."

I considered that and nodded. Most of those things did sound pretty fun or useful. "Any cons?"

"Hmm. Not seeing colors." He gestured in front of him. "It's all curious tones of gray."

I pursed my lips, agreeing. "That would be hard."

"What color are your eyes?"

I didn't know what I had expected him to say next, but it wasn't that. "Um, green."

"Green," he muttered, looking down at his hands, a tentative smile lifting one corner of his mouth. "Well-hydrated grass green, or mung bean green?"

"Are those my only two options?" I deadpanned.

His eyes flicked up, a teasing glint in their dark depths. "It's the mung bean green, isn't it?"

I rolled my eyes. "I prefer moss green."

I wasn't quite sure, but he mumbled something that sounded like, "Me too." But before I could ask him, he lifted his head, lips puckering in thought. I averted my eyes to the hem of my sweater, not wanting to get caught staring at his mouth. "Another con would be the strange urge to play with yarn. The affinity for shiny things; also quite annoying."

I chuckled at his tone, which oozed genuine displeasure.

"You have no idea," he insisted. "It's a compulsion I will happily be rid of."

I glanced up, nodding in mock empathy. "Do these urges only persist in cat form or..." I inquired with a chuckle, finding the loose thread on the sleeve of my sweater and giving it a flick. It had unraveled a lot since I had first noticed it, shortly after my mom had bought it for me.

Shroding rolled his eyes, muttering, "You say I'm trouble," but his eyes were glued to the string.

I wiggled my brows, giving my arm a little shake as I held the thread out to him. He looked like he might actually take the bait, but then, with a laugh of his own, he tossed a fistful of straw at me.

"Hey!" I flinched, covering my head. I shook the dry silage from my hair and shirt with a grin. "Well, I'm sure it will be nice to be a person again," I encouraged, maybe a little too hopeful.

"Sure," he agreed, helping me pull the straw from my clothes. "I just hope I won't have to relearn how to speak or walk on two legs." He gestured to his bent knees.

"That would be unfortunate. For a small fee, I could be your tutor," I offered wryly.

"Well, then I have nothing to fear." He smirked. "Speaking of tutoring..." He stood and offered me his hand. "I do believe I promised more training."

"Right," I agreed, sliding my hand into his.

CHAPTER 10
Warmth

I had been so wet and cold when I went to sleep, but when I woke, beads of sweat collected on my forehead.

"Ugh," I groaned, opening my eyes to see the gray sky still overhead. Heavy fabric dropped from my shoulder to the ground. "Huh?" Puzzled, I looked at the thick coat on the ground. It was a dark green with a thick gray fur lining. The outside was stiff and structured but had a plushness to it from the fur on the inside. I felt the chill of the morning and quickly scooped the coat up. I delighted in its warmth, poking my arms through. It looked almost new, save for multiple sets of puncture marks that littered the collar and sleeves.

"Sorry about that. I tried not to damage it." Shroding stirred on the mat next to me.

"Did you..." I could not hide my surprise. "Where did you get this?"

"I stole it from a nearby town after you fell asleep."

I stifled a laugh, imagining him carrying such a bulky item in his mouth.

"Isn't it risky for you to go to town, especially at night? What if the moon lit up your fur and someone saw you?"

"The storm covered the sky. Besides, I don't give off the king's power. I'm connected to it, sure, but I'm just a cat," he assured me.

I worried my lip, not liking him putting himself at risk even if he actually was perfectly safe.

"Haya, I have been a cat for two hundred years and have taken care of myself well enough. You don't need to worry about me."

But I did, and a part of me thought I always would, even when he became a strong, capable king someday. Friends worried about friends, had their backs. "Thank you," I breathed, grateful, but also very conflicted. He had not slept again, traveled who knows how far to get me a coat and still managed to keep the fire going all night and have a whole conversation with me in the other dimension. He was taking care of me in every way he could. "Thank you" didn't quite feel like enough.

"It might be a bit big, but you can use it as a blanket at night that way." He sounded very proud of himself, like he had made a real effort coming to this conclusion. My grin grew wider.

"It's perfect." I beamed, and for just a moment in his cat eyes I could see Shroding, the man, smiling back at me.

Shroding was curled into my side just like the night he'd bounced into my room like he owned the place and had lain on my bed like it was the most natural thing for him to do. I had glowered at his audacity then, but now I wondered.

I shifted to my side, running my fingers over his damp fur. He twisted eyes meeting mine, the iridescence they normally held was dimmed in the gray of the day. "That night you came into my room..." I began, "was it the first time?"

He looked sheepish, as sheepish as a cat could look, anyway. He sat up and walked over to the embers of the fire he had tended to while I slept. "No." He paused... "I had been checking on you every night, since the day on the dandelion hill." I smiled at his use of Theo's and my childhood name for the hill. "It wasn't till the day when you opened Theo's present that I made it a requirement."

I sat up, rubbing the sleep from my eyes. "The blanket with the stars?"

"Yes, it was another sign." He chuckled lightly, tossing some of the straw on the embers, igniting a new spark. "Another reason to look at you and hope I had found the way to become human again."

I recalled how he'd curled up on the star pattern. "I thought it was odd that you lay down specifically on the design, but how was that another sign?"

"That blanket was specially commissioned at my father's request when I was born. There were only two made, one for my childhood room and one for the king's chambers."

"You mean that blanket was yours?" I gaped.

"Yes..."

"What do the stars mean?" I had always wondered why there were three.

"They represented my family; my mother, father and me," he said, sadness and pride in his voice.

King Roark must have really loved Elina and his son. "That's really beautiful." Even though Shroding was a secret, the king had something so beautiful made to remember and honor his family. "How do you think it ended up on the farm?"

"My father was a clever man," he praised, shoving a fresh log onto the growing flames with his nose. "But to be honest, I have no idea. I just knew it was a clue... No, it was a confirmation. He must have known that once I saw it I would be assured I had found the path he intended me to follow. How he orchestrated it... " His tail swished, and he tilted his head in a "I have no idea" kind of way.

"I'm sorry it was destroyed in the fire."

His iridescent eyes flashed in the warm light of the campfire. "It's okay, I have a feeling I'll see it again. I don't think anyone would touch my father's chambers in the palace, so the second one is probably still there."

My heart stirred at the hope in his voice, and tears threatened my eyes. The promise I had made in the other dimension gave me strength. I would help him no matter what. I would make sure he saw his home again. I might not be able to go back to the life I'd had. I might not be able to bring back the people we'd lost, but I could do this much, right? I could make sure he got to keep that one memento of his father. I could make sure he returned to the life he had before. "I know you will," I fervently agreed. "I will make sure you do."

"Thanks, Haya." He rose onto his hind legs. The feeling of sandpaper swiping my cheek made me flinch. He had given me a cat kiss, and I would have been embarrassed if not for the hint of tears in his eyes.

I pet him behind the ear. "I should go see if there's any dry wood left outside," I said, clearing my throat. I could feel Shroding's eyes follow me as I stood and walked out of the shed.

The tears lingered in my eyes, but I did not want Shroding to see me cry again. I had thought I had done a decent job hiding my pain, but after last night I was beginning to think I had not been as convincing as I'd hoped. Shroding was always watching me, as if waiting for me to snap again. As if I were some fragile child who would just cry and cry without Mommy or Daddy. But to his four hundred years of life, I *was* a child. I had thought I would seem petty and small to him. But through his show of affection for a childhood blanket, I understood Shroding was hurting just as much, if not more, and this realization gave me strength. I didn't want him to be in pain, but the fact he was made me less alone in mine.

I tucked another branch under my arm, my eyes burning with unshed tears. I swallowed the lump in my throat. I would not give up, I would not give in to the sorrow again. Shroding was so strong. Sure, he'd had years to build that strength, but something told me it hadn't taken him years to become strong enough to accept his mission. Now I had a mission, and once it was complete I could crumble and fall apart.

Perhaps by the time my mission was done, I would not need to fall apart at all. I would reunite with my mom, and we would start over with the permanent burdens and scars on our hearts. But we would begin again. I would rise up and overcome this.

The sound of my father's deep laugh rang in my ears. Theo's comforting arm over my shoulder would be my pain and joy. I would not lose the memories, and I would not be afraid to relive them. Each time I shared my memories of them, I would be honoring them. I would not let their deaths be for nothing. I would free Shroding and help him rid our world of Skithian for good.

This war would end.

I would do everything in my power to bring peace, or I would die trying. This would be my strength, because in Shroding's unshed tears I realized my own strength. A strength in me not tied to the king's power or my family. The power of choice, a power so strong, a power decided by me. This would be my strength because, though I had not chosen this path, I could still choose how I would walk it. I could still choose what my perception was going to be on this journey; one of fear or one of determined purpose.

I waited till my tears had ebbed before returning to the shed.

I had done my best to shield the bundle of firewood in my arms from the steady rain turning to ice. I had gathered enough for at least two nights, even though I was sure Shroding would have us move on before then, especially with Callum on our trail. Though I hoped we had lost him in the storm.

When I entered the small space, Shroding sat gazing up at the hole in the roof again as if he could will the precipitation to stop. The fire he had started had fizzled out in the damp air.

"It just started to sleet," I said, holding the bundle in my arms, careful to keep it dry as I squeezed through the doorway.

"Yes, and what's worse is—" He was cut off by a loud rumble and crack.

"A thunderstorm?" I gasped.

"Yes, well, it's called a thundersnow. We need to stay put a little longer till it passes. Neither of us would like getting hit by lightning."

I dropped the load, shoving half of it under a layer of straw to protect it. The other half of the sticks I balanced against one another in a pyramid as Shroding had done the other night. "I meant to ask you... when do you sleep, if you are keeping the fire going all night?"

"Cat naps?" he said jokingly, but I knew he was trying to avoid the question. He was barely sleeping. I knew the cats in my barn had slept well over the human-recommended eight hours. But so far on our journey, this morning was the only time I had seen him close his eyes.

"Ha, ha." I gave in half-heartedly, trying not to let my concern show. He had enough to manage without the burden of my fussing over him. Warm flames slowly licked the kindling till the whole fire was catching.

I scooted back onto the bedroll. My stomach growled in competition with the thunder, and I bit my lip, embarrassed.

"Got that covered." He pulled over a satchel holding a small loaf of bread and numerous cheeses. "I meant to give this to you earlier."

"More contraband?" I laughed, taking the cheese and bread from the pouch. I still had food from Callum's pack as well.

"You needn't worry, I got the name of the family. I will be repaying them handsomely once I'm... me again." He gave a slight gesture to his cat physique, and I chuckled.

I took the food, looking at the fang marks, which matched the punctures in my coat. I raised my eyebrows.

"What did you expect? I don't have thumbs." He sank to his haunches, his tail wrapping around his paws. "I won't be offended if you eat around it." He looked away, letting me do as I pleased.

I ate half the bread and a few slices of cheese, hunger winning out over whatever reservation I should have had, knowing the food had been in his mouth at some point.

We listened to the roar and flash of thunder and lightning, the fire snapping and popping as time passed slowly. Though I had slept already, I found the sounds, coupled with Shroding's purring and the warm coat, were enough to carry me to sleep once more.

Only the howling in the distance seemed displaced in the lulling sounds around me.

CHAPTER 11

Run Away With Me

My eyes could have only been closed a second when I heard Shroding calling me.

"Haya!"

"What?" I sat up, confused by the crack of hail on the shed roof. White pearls fell from the ceiling, bouncing off my coat and onto the moss floor, like some kind of pellucid jewel on a bed of green.

"We have to go." Shroding kicked dirt over the flames in an attempt to put it out. I registered his urgency and diverted my attention from the hailstones.

My mind raced to understand his words. Had the Grieving caught up to us? Had Callum found us through the storm?

My heart skipped a few beats, and I jumped to help him douse the fire.

"No," he thought angrily. "We are out of time."

"What is it?" I asked softly, but the thunder drowned out my question, and the flash that followed cast ominous shadows through the wall I had patched.

Before he could speak, I heard them; the growls and wet snuffles of dogs.

"Marauders... and their pets." Shroding shivered a little, and I wondered if the "cats don't like dogs" stereotype applied to him too. I moved to the rusted door and peered through a narrow split in the wood. I could make out a slender figure covered head to toe in thick furs. His face was shrouded by a black mask bearing two white dots under the left eye, and the only part of his face visible was his mouth, which was lifted in a sneer.

Two black hounds flanked the masked man and sniffed the air as they moved through freshly fallen snow. They barked twice.

"It's a girl. And she is alone." A man I could not see from my vantage point said somewhere to the left of the shed. I bit my lip to stop from gasping. How did they know? And not for the first time I wondered how close I had to be for someone to feel my vibrations. Were there just two of them or more on the way?

"Looks like she has herself a horse too." The masked man responded, leaning down to inspect the snow. "Our find just keeps getting better and better."

"Haya," Shroding said, his paw resting on my hand. "These men don't have the gift, but they will kill you if they find you."

I flinched at his certainty.

"They have a darkness about them. I think they are working for Skithian."

Enemies this deep into the mountains? They should have been caught on the Bezer Plains when they traveled up from Golan, unless these men weren't Golanites at all. What if there was corruption within the very people of Shamar?

"So what do we do?"

"We have to run," he said simply.

"What about the camp supplies?" I glanced at the bedroll, and as petty as it was, the snowfall only reinforced that I didn't want to sleep on the freezing-cold ground.

"We will have to forget it. Now get as low as possible and get to your horse. Etienne ran away before they got here, but you can follow his tracks to the left of the shed."

I nodded.

"I'll distract them while you get away."

Panic bubbled in my chest. "I don't like separating." How would we find each other?

"I will find you." He spoke with such fervor that I turned to look at him. Though he was not looking at me, I could see the unwavering commitment in his eyes. I could sense his absolute resolve that he would find me, no matter what.

"I will go this way." I pointed to the hole in the wall.

"Hurry."

I pushed the barrier down at the same time the door clattered open, rusty hinges shattering at the force. Shroding growled, launching himself at the man as I pressed into the stones on the outside of the shed, doing my best to skirt the perimeter. I ignored the wild scream of the marauder and the snarls of the dogs coming to his aid, hoping Shroding was not on the receiving end of their rage, but even if he was, I had to believe he would get out unscathed.

Taking a shaky breath, I peered around the outside of the shed. The snow-laden ground made for an easy canvas to read. Seeing the way was clear, I made my escape.

I could no longer see the shed as I sprinted through the trees, finding the hoofprints Etienne had left in the snow.

"No you don't!" a gruff voice, far closer than I expected,

yelled over the steady thumps of falling hail and low, groaning thunder.

I cried out as the man slammed into my back, knocking me into the pitted slush of the ground. Cold ice sprayed my face. I struggled, bucking until I was able to get enough purchase to thrust my elbow back, connecting with his face and pushing him off.

I turned on my knees to see the same man from before. The black mask cracked at the side, a jagged line split the wood upward, stopping under the white dots below his eye.

"Quit squealing already," he ordered, rubbing his jaw.

I scrambled to crawl away when his hand, cold and rough, struck out against my cheek, tossing me off my knees and into the muddied snow. The impact was rattling, and for a moment I could only see spots.

"She has a beast with her!" the other man called, limping towards us with only one of the dogs in tow. The man who'd slapped me grabbed me under the armpits and hoisted me onto my feet, my back to his front as he locked us together. The snowscape spun as I tried to blink away the dizziness and look for Shroding. Where was he?

"Don't worry about me." Shroding's voice was soft, pained, and far away.

In an instant my vision cleared, and I screamed in my mind. "Where are you? Are you hurt?!"

"Ugh! I'm coming," he panted, and terror filled me as I saw blood dripping from the approaching dog's mouth.

"Little pet, lost in the woods," the limping man said, jerking my chin to make me look at him. He wore a mask as well, but his only had one dot. The marauder holding me pulled back, squeezing my shoulder with his forearms. I winced but squared my chin and rocked forward, spitting in the face of the man before me.

He scowled, whipping my ire with disgust before encroaching further into my space.

I had to think. If they didn't have the gift, then they wouldn't know that I did. Recalling what Shroding had said about drawing out the king's power, I focused on the few times back at the farm I had done it. I just needed enough to break free and get Shroding to safety.

"Haya, don't!"

But it was the only thing I could do to save him, save us both. So in my mind's eye I envisioned the power moving in me like a swirl of strings, rolling and flowing together, building inside me, tingling along my fingertips. It came easily, as if it desperately wanted me to call it out. So I did, letting it flow through my hands, arms, till it filled my body.

"She has a bit of fight. Let her know what she can expect from us in return." The man holding me shifted as he spoke into my ear.

"She might be worth selling to the camps, but we should try her out first." The man's face came in close, and before I could register what he was doing, his lips closed over mine, while the other man laughed in my ear. His sweat and stubble scraped over my skin, lips dry and unyielding against mine.

I screamed, trying desperately to break the contact as understanding dawned on me. These men were slave traders.

"Haya!" Shroding's voice broke through my thoughts.

"Stay back," I begged him.

"By the Strings!" he growled, and I knew he was running into the fray to attack the men despite my warning.

But I couldn't risk him getting hurt more, so I closed my

eyes, blocking everything out. Just as the man's tongue forced its way into my mouth, I bit down, hard.

As soon as the man jerked away, I shoved back on the marauder behind me, knowing he could take it and not buckle under my weight as I tucked my knees to my chest between me and the monster who had just assaulted me. I forced as much power as I could manage into my legs and kicked.

Waves of vibration rippled around the point of impact, and a sound like a thunderclap burst through the woods, shaking trees and knocking me and the other man to the ground. The other man flew through the air, vanishing into the stormy woods, but not before I saw blood pouring from his mouth.

"Haya!" Shroding ran to my side, teeth bared and claws out as he jumped the snarling dog charging straight for me. I rolled away just in time for Shroding to rip his claws into it. The dog roared, teeth snapping at Shroding's shoulder. They rolled in the snow, biting and scratching. Blood left a trail across the white—whose, I wasn't sure. Their scuffle took them a few feet away and into the trees.

I tried to breathe as revulsion coursed through me. All I wanted to do was take fistfuls of snow and wash out my mouth, but we were not safe yet, so I staggered to my feet. The masked man with the two dots was faster and rose to stand over me.

"You have the gift!" he howled in rage. "I will make a fortune off you." Then he lunged at me, a knife in his hand he had not had before.

The booming of hooves reached my ears as a white horse and a rider with golden hair barreled towards the marauder.

"Get down!" Callum shouted, his sword poised to strike.

I dropped into the snow, hearing the blade cut through flesh, and a wet thump hit the ground beside me.

I shivered, unable to move.

"Don't look," Callum ordered grimly. I didn't need to be told twice.

"Haya..." Shroding whispered, and with that simple word I knew he was in trouble. In a flash I was up, running in the direction he and the dog had gone.

"Hey!" Callum called, but I ignored him, finding Shroding on shaky legs behind a tree, the dog's body bloody and limp on the ground next to him. His chest rose and fell, white puffs of air leaving his nose in short bursts.

"Where are you hurt?" I panicked.

"There's no time," he panted, darting away from where Callum ran towards us.

Like a Seraph sent by the Creator of Strings himself to save us, Etienne appeared. He cut off Callum, rearing up and coming down hard, heaving dirt and slush into the air like a wall.

I grabbed the reins and hoisted myself onto his back, but not before Callum grabbed the hood of my coat, pulling me backwards. The present of warmth I did not want to let go of was almost enough to pull me clean off Etienne's back, but Shroding wouldn't want that. He would want me to escape, not linger just because of a coat. With some effort I ripped my arms free of the warm fur and threw myself forward across Etienne's back.

The horse needed no further incentive, and with a huff and one last kick he set off running into the storm after Shroding.

CHAPTER 12

Separated

The trees looked eerie now that I was alone. The spindly gray branches seemed to reach out to me like the teeth or claws of some hungry creature.

Etiennne had taken off through the woods, sensing the danger or my fear. After riding some distance, I realized I had lost Shroding and slowed my pace to look around. Which way had Shroding gone?

"Shroding?" I called again and again.

The blur of trees and swirling snow from the storm left me disoriented. I had no idea where I was or what direction I had just run off in. I mentally kicked myself. How was I going to find Shroding again? Had I just put us off course? Had I gone in the opposite direction of Tyndale?

I found myself wishing I had gone camping with Micah and Theo when I was little. I had zero wilderness survival skills, and the sun, from what I could tell through the overcast sky, was setting, taking with it the barely-above-freezing temperature.

I shivered, my clothes completely soaked through from the fight in the snow.

I looked around, walking Etienne in circles before giving up on pinpointing a direction to go. A rush of tired dread stirred in the pit of my stomach. I tried not to let panic set in and make me do something stupid. I needed to think.

I got off Etienne and inspected the ground. The hailstorm had passed, leaving only faint traces of its presence in the snow around the hoofprints. I could follow Etienne's tracks back the way I'd come or trust that Shroding would use them to find me. That is, if the fresh snowfall did not cover them first.

I pulled some baby hairs out of my head and stuck them into the hoofprint in case Shroding was trying to follow my scent. He was a cat, after all—that was something he could do, right? I didn't exactly know the full extent of his abilities; he was a bit different from the average house cat.

Mounting the saddle, I reasoned I should find somewhere suitable to wait out the storm and attempt to make a fire if I could find wood dry enough—and if I was able to make fire without Shroding's help, which I was not sure I could.

I wandered for a while, stopping every few yards to pull out more baby hair and press them into Etienne's tracks.

"Shroding, wherever you are, find me please..." I sniffed, my nose cold and wet like a puppy. I rubbed the tip, attempting to warm it, but my fingers were so cold I could no longer feel them. Between that and my chattering teeth, I knew I would not fare well if I did not find some shelter soon. The reins slipped between my chapped hands as I struggled to grip them.

Glancing around, I saw an old tree with a wide base and a low, swooping branch that twisted to the ground in a crescent shape. I dismounted and shuffled my way over, then slumped down into its cradle.

I was too cold to sleep, but even if I could, I was a tired that sleeping would not remedy. My mind reeled again from the events of the last month, and I marveled at how I could come so far just to die lost in the mountains.

I convulsed with another shiver and curled up tighter in a ball. Far off in the distance, wolves howled. Nothing like a little hypothermia and fear of being ripped to shreds to lift spirits. As if my luck and hopes for survival were not bad enough, something cold and wet splashed my face. Rain. My scent would get washed away with the rain. The bracing wind rustled the leaves, picking loose the last of the dead foliage from the trees and carrying them away. I pondered how the forest could look so beautiful by day and so deadly by night.

I needed a plan, and waiting for my furry friend just wasn't going to cut it. I tried to stand, but something seemed to root me to the tree. If I left and the rain washed my trail and scent away, Shroding might never find me. I needed to get higher up. I needed to see better to find my way out of this forest to a town or shelter, but my legs just wouldn't move. The ground was getting a fresh dusting of sleet, and though it was cold I didn't feel as cold anymore, but I was not sure if that was a good thing or not.

My head lolled on the tree trunk. A small gecko poked its head out of a knot in the tree. I stared at its yellow reptilian eyes. A strange foreboding passed over me. I closed my eyes and turned my head away from the small creature.

Yellow eyes. Also reptilian, set in a cold, sickly looking face. A creature of some sort, a memory or thought I wasn't sure of flicked in my mind. It was elusive, like holding sand in a fist. Then it was gone.

My ankles were swollen, and my inner thighs ached from riding. I was getting a bad headache, and though I didn't want to admit it, I wasn't going to find shelter anytime soon. Still, I needed to keep moving. If I stayed in this spot, the elements would win.

Etienne walked up alongside the tree, the saddle within reach. Weakly, I gripped the horn of the saddle, and pulled myself over till my belly lay atop and my face rested in Etienne's wet mane. He gave a tired neigh but began moving. I gripped the horn, determined to stay on despite my numb hands.

The snow collected on my back, but I could not raise my head. I swung in and out of consciousness, the only sound in the snowy night the crunching of Etienne's hooves in the snow.

I did not dream, I just drifted. Flashes of strange things passed through my mind. Pieces of the memories Shroding had tried to share with me, and mixes of memories with Theo and my father. I was at the farm, and I was happy. It was the time for the Celebration of Strings, and I was waiting for Dad to open a gift I'd made for him. Then I was in the palace, watching Shroding turn into a silver-and-black cat. Fragments of my own memories on the dandelion hill with Micah rolled through my mind as well as the howl of wolves rang in the distance.

———

Pocket Dimension

I sat up slowly. A fallen tree was my shelter. I reached up to touch it, amazed at its thickness. It would take three of me to wrap around it. Gingerly I rose, watching out for my head, as the space was a lot smaller than it seemed lying down. I must have stopped and fallen asleep here, but I had no memory of any of that.

A small pile of wood lay on the ground just outside the covering of the fallen tree. A firepit, but no fire.

I remember being very cold, lying across Etienne's back. The horse was nowhere in sight. I was in the rip, the darkness creeping in.

Shaking my head to clear it, I called for Shroding. I felt his presence before I saw him. Everything became bright.

It had not been that long since we saw each other last, but something about his gaze made me a little self-conscious.

He leaned on the tree, his body tense, eyes flashing with an intensity that made me uneasy.

I opened my mouth to greet him and snapped it shut when he strode over to me, falling to his knees and wrapping his arms so tight around me I squeaked.

"By the Strings," he repeated over and over and over in his mind.

"Shroding?" I reached up, wrapping my arms around him in return, patting his back in a reassuring way. What had him so spooked? Was it because of the attack? Because we'd gotten separated? What could I say to comfort him?

But before I could speak he asked, "How are you feeling?"

"Strange."

He pulled back, looking me over.

I glanced at my hands, which were numb. In fact, most of me felt odd, like all my parts were not attached to my body.

He cupped my hands in his. "Can you feel this?" he whispered. The tenderness in his voice had me melting. Then I realized I couldn't feel his hands at all.

"No..." I whispered back, searching his eyes for a clue as to what was wrong.

"I found your trail and then followed the scent. The storm made it hard to be certain which way you went. It took longer than I would have liked to find you. I'm sorry."

"For what?" I asked.

"For running off, for not waiting for you. I-I panicked." He sounded ashamed.

"Why?" I wondered.

"Callum was right there, and I was injured and..." He shook his head disgustedly. "By the Strings, I'm such a coward. I should have been sure you were right behind me. I should have checked, waited for you." He ran his fingers through his hair, the dark strands sticking out. "When I found you, you were delirious and soaked to the bone, and it's—"

"Shh," I soothed, reaching up to fix his hair. Though I could see my fingers sliding through his hair, there was no sensation to it.

He breathed out shakily. He had been really worried about me, and my heart squeezed, delighted.

Taking my hands back in his, he repeated, "I'm sorry."

"You found me, that's all that matters." I lifted my chin, smiled and tried to squeeze his hands.

"I'm doing the best I can to keep you warm, but you're freezing."

Was that why I could not feel his hands holding mine? I didn't feel cold in the pocket, though. I looked at the pile of wood. He had probably tried to make a fire but couldn't without the king's power.

"How does it work, you being in both dimensions?"

He thought for a moment, his lips parting then closing. "It's like physically I'm there, but spiritually I'm here" He patted his hand on his knee. "I see both at the same time. I'm not in two places at once, per se. I'm both here and there, even right now. It's hard to explain." I waited for him to find the right words, watching how when they came to him, his face lit up. "At first it was disorienting. A lot of the time I had to keep my eyes closed in the physical world to fully see in this dimension, but now I can process both at the same time. I can move between both sets of eyes, both sets of senses. Like turning your attention to someone talking in another room but also still hearing the person in the room you're in. They are divided but easy to shift between. Though my cat senses are a bit more overpowering."

"It sounds difficult to process. I can't even imagine."

He looked over at me, his eyes dark but emitting the same iridescence as a moonstone. For a moment I forgot he was a prince, and I stared back, searching the darkness, wondering how he could make me feel so light. He always seemed to be lighting up this dimension. Making me warm, safe. "I have had time to practice."

"What do you see now? As a cat?" I asked, looking around the shelter.

He scooped me up in his arms and carried me into the back corner of the tree and set me down. His arms were still wrapped around me as he spoke. "You're leaning here, knees tucked up under your chin, holding your braid between your hands as you are in this dimension."

I awkwardly let go of my braid. I hadn't realized I was holding it. "And you?"

He shifted so my back was against his chest, his body curled around mine like a blanket. His arms wrapped around me like I was something precious he needed to protect. He had lost me, and I was the key to him becoming human again—of course I was precious to him.

In my confusion and relief and the fact I couldn't feel the cold, I had not noticed I was not wearing my knit sweater. I gasped, and I covered myself with my arms. Thankfully my chest was still covered by my undergarments. But what in the Strings had caused me to lose my shirt?

"Where is my—" I couldn't finish the thought as his chin rested on my bare shoulder.

"I'm sorry for that too. It was the only thing I could get off. I'm hoping it will be dry by the time you wake up." His words did not comfort me, as it implied he had tried to take my other clothes off as well.

"Why in the world did you..." I sputtered, mortified.

"Survival 101: Stay dry. If not, then get dry. You needed to get out of those wet clothes. I stayed close to you as well, hoping to maintain your temperature, but my fur was wet. I dug through the pack from Callum and used the blanket and gloves he had, as they were dry. Etienne blocked the entrance, preventing the wind from hitting us," he explained, not sounding the least bit embarrassed. He was all clinical explanation.

I didn't know what to say. Shroding had taken my shirt off... as a cat. How absurdly bizarre.

"Did you have a lot of experience in the woods growing up?"

"I may not have been allowed to wander freely in the

castle, but the woods... That was a different story altogether. Camping was a staple activity in my family. In fact, it is family tradition. On my eighth birthday my father and the court decided to send me on a monthlong trip with my best friends. We were to apply everything we had learned about survival. It was to prepare us for the King's Challenge, which I would do after my fifteenth birthday."

"The King's Challenge? I've never heard of it."

"Not surprising, only the king's court was aware of it since they invented it. The details would even be kept from the current king as a way to keep him from interfering."

"What happens during the challenge?"

"Don't know. I never got to complete it, I became a cat."

"Oh, right," I said sheepishly. "So the monthlong trip was like a pretest?"

"Exactly." He smiled.

"What happened?"

He settled into a comfortable position, leaning us back against the tree. Arms still tight around me he tucked his chin onto my shoulder and started to tell me about how they'd each been given a pack of supplies. Then they were separated, left to find each other in the woods.

I smiled, seeing the child in him come to the surface as he gestured with his hands. The memory was somber but clearly exciting for him to share.

"When we found each other, we had enough supplies for two weeks."

I tilted my head. "That's only half the time, how did you survive the other two weeks?"

"Well, we had a few hiccups along the way. After we made a plan, we oriented ourselves and found the best path on our map to get to the castle. As the future king, I was to *lead the group, but it was hard; I had never led anything. They were my best friends, and I had never made them treat me as a king. They were always free to say what they thought or share ideas with me, but out in the wild we needed a leader, a hierarchy to follow among us, but the hierarchy was a mess. We fought almost all the time. We didn't know how to work together in a life or death situation. I began to realize why my father had me do the pretest, as you called it, with them. I had to learn to trust them, to learn how to lead them as a king. We had to change what we grew up knowing."*

"So what happened?" I asked, sliding down the cot to join him on the floor.

"An unexpected storm flooded our camp and washed away the animal tracks we were using to navigate back to the capital. The herd we had been following was a pack that always stayed near the capital for mating at that time of the year. We had planned to follow them out of the forest. We didn't think we were more than four days away from the Romath."

"What did you do with the tracks gone?"

"Well, we panicked for a while. Then we were attacked by a troop from Golan. They didn't know who we were, or they would have killed us on the spot. Asher and Logan had gone scouting ahead when we were ambushed. Callum had tried to defend me, and in doing so they took a special interest in me. Callum couldn't protect me then, and he seemed to beat himself up for it long after. The troop had planned to kill me when Logan showed up. He told them to take our supplies and spare my life. They took what we had left of our supplies but didn't want to spare me. Logan then convinced them I would be an asset to them if they took me back to Golan."

The horrified look on my face made Shroding laugh. "How can you laugh right now? What happened?"

"Trust me, I wasn't laughing when it happened." He put his hand over mine. "I survived, I'm here now, aren't I..." He half smiled and shrugged. "Well, sort of."

I frowned, waiting for him to continue.

"They beat Logan and left both Callum and him for dead. They took me, and for three days I was sure I would never see my father or Romath ever again." He smiled, reaching over to my face, his thumb rubbing the furrow between my brows. "Relax, Haya. Relax." I exhaled. "I'm not going to finish telling you if you keep stressing out like this."

"Fine, I promise to be moderately indifferent to your pain from now on," I said imperiously.

"Very good." He laughed. "Well, after three days the group from Golan was attacked by a pack of wild cats. I stole one of their horses and took off in the night. Using the stars as my guide, I found my way to a town on the border of Golan and Shamar. As luck would have it, I found Asher and Callum there. They had wanted to go looking for me but needed to get supplies. Logan had said it was better to get back to the palace or find a troop of our own soldiers so word could get to the king about what had happened. Callum and Asher knew that would be the end of it, we would have failed the test by asking for help. They knew that was the last thing I wanted."

"So Logan just left you?"

"He thought he was doing the right thing at the time."

"Still, Callum and Asher were going to fight a bunch of soldiers from Golan to get you back. That's incredibly brave, if not a little stupid."

"Well, they thought it was the right thing to do at the time," he answered diplomatically.

"And you? What did you want to do then?"

"I was relieved I hadn't been sold off as a slave in Golan. But I decided we needed to get to Logan and finish the test. So we looked for him. We spied around the town to see if we could get news of him, but we were hungry, tired and honestly a bit over all of it. We spent two days in the town with no luck finding Logan. On the third day we overheard that a troop from Romath was going to cross the border to Golan. We knew if Logan was anywhere, it had to be with them, so we hurried to find them." He took a deep breath and sighed.

"Well?" I asked impatiently.

"You're doing it again." He smirked, reaching over to rub my brow.

"Well, stop dragging it out and tell me the end of it!" I whined.

"We found him. He was following the troop. He had not asked for their help yet. We were so relieved, we never even bothered to ask him why. We regrouped and followed the troop's path back to Romath. We hunted and found water along the way. There may have been a small run-in with a wild boar. In the end we all made it to the castle alive."

"A wild boar, oh yeah, sure, of course." I nodded, failing at indifference. "Remind me to never doubt your wilderness survival skills."

"Gladly." He smirked again.

"So, you tried to make a fire?"

He nodded. "For hours you slept but did not call to me. I was beginning to worry you might not wake up."

"I must be getting better, if I was able to move dimensions again?"

"That's my thought precisely."

"Is there a way I can help you make a fire without being awake?"

He shifted me in his arms so I could see his face. "No, you would need to be like I am, connected to both the physical and spiritual dimension to access it. Here you are only in the spirit; there is no way for you to use the power here and have it come out of your physical form..." He paused, looking down at the dirt, his face pensive. "Actually. I could maybe be a conduit here as well." His eyes brightened as they flashed up to mine. "Want to try it?"

I too lit up at his excitement, but also at the idea of getting my shirt back on. He might actually be unfazed by my lack of clothes, but I definitely was not. Every breath I took had my chest rising and falling, making me achingly self-conscious.

"Absolutely."

CHAPTER 13

Something New

POCKET DIMENSION

After a few attempts that failed spectacularly—one so bad Shroding had to lie down to stave off nausea—we successfully transferred the power.

Though the fire did not appear in the pocket dimension, I slowly began to have sensation in my hands and toes again.

"I hung your sweater near the fire. It should dry quickly," he offered, collapsing next to me in the dirt. "I'm exhausted." He huffed, lying back and throwing his arm over his eyes. His lips parted as a shudder passed through him.

"Are you going to be okay?"

"Yeah, it's just like last time. I'll just rest in the physical dimension for a while."

"You can do that and still be conscious here?" I mused, bewildered.

He snorted, peering up at me from behind his arm. "It's no different than what you are doing right now."

I pursed my lips in chagrin.

"So what is the plan? I get better, and we take off into the storm again?"

"The skies are clear now. It was a fast-moving storm. They are all like that in this part of the mountains. We do need to find food and fresh water. That will be our next step after you wake up."

"Do you think Callum is still following our trail?"

"He was the best tracker of the four of us, so I imagine he is not far behind," he mumbled mostly to himself.

"What happened between you two? I mean, he did save my life."

Shroding was quiet for a long time, and I hated that I couldn't see his expression. Was it too painful and sad for him, like it was for me, to talk about the people he'd lost?

"Asher, Callum and Logan." His voice was wistful as he broke the silence. "They were picked to be my future general, commander, and court leader. It was my father's desire that we grow up together as a way to secure loyalty and kinship among the future leaders of Shamar. They were going to fight alongside me to make a new future. It was good logic even if the execution didn't go as planned."

"What do you mean? Because you became a cat?"

He shook his head. "It doesn't matter. They were my brothers—still are, for my part, so I guess my father's intention came true after all," he mused.

If he still saw them as brothers, why had he sounded so fearful when Callum had shown up? Why had he hidden? If Callum was supposed to be loyal to the king, why did Shroding want nothing to do with him?

I was about to ask as much when Shroding continued. "Earlier, I mentioned that you had seen Callum before."

I nodded.

"Do you remember a dream from a while ago, a man with golden hair and gray eyes?" he supplied, waiting for my recollection of the image. At the mention of gray eyes I instantly knew exactly what he was talking about.

"The dream I had about the journal and a cat in a bathtub. That was— Wait, how do you know about that dream? It wasn't a part of this dimension. Was it?" It had been jumbled and nonsensical the way dreams normally were.

"I knew you would remember him. He's handsome, right? Hard to forget." He laughed a little, and I fought the urge to disagree with him. Sure, Callum was handsome, but Shroding's face the day he showed up in that first dream and carried me out of the barn was on a whole other level. My cheeks warmed, and Shroding laughed harder, no doubt misunderstanding my flush. "That dream—and you're right, it was just a dream—was my first attempt at putting images in your mind. Before that I had only tried talking to you via our connection. Of course I didn't factor in how your subconscious would change the images. It didn't exactly go as I had planned. I only wanted to show you some of my memories in the hopes it would nudge you in my direction a little more. Like I said before, you needed to find the truth out for yourself, but I couldn't help but encourage things a bit on my part."

I was still reeling from the idea that he'd put his memories in my head as he continued. "Callum always watched our backs as kids. Or at least he had, even from people we should have been able to trust." His tone grew dark. "Even from each other."

"What happened to make you doubt his loyalty?" Had they encountered each other before, while Shroding was a cat? That had to be it; how else would Shroding have known what

Callum looked like as an adult if they were all kids together before the transformation?

"Before I became a cat, my father's general told me I would need to find the king's power to become human again, but only when it was the right time. I had no idea when the right time was, and no one gave me any clues to follow. When I became a cat, I woke up in the woods, alone. I wandered for a long time, exploring everything I couldn't see when I was a secret in the castle. There were a few times, after the change, when I stayed in the major cities. I had thought it would be beneficial for whoever got the king's power. That it would make it easier for whoever it was to find me, but... it was then I learned there had been a betrayal in the king's court. That it was indeed easier to find me, but not by the people who might help me."

"Betrayal?"

"One of my friends attempted to have me killed when I was in one of the cities. He had turned to Skithian when my father died. Perhaps even beforehand, it's hard to say." Shroding worked his jaw. "After that, I stayed away from most towns and cities. I would only venture to the outskirts of very small villages. It got easier to be a cat, and after being held captive by one of my closest friends, I decided to give myself over to the animal I had become, and the wild became my home."

"You don't know who it was who tried to have you killed?"

He shook his head. "Asher and I were the same age. Callum and Logan a year older. Asher and I looked a lot alike, until recently. I heard when he got the gift his eyes turned blue. Anyway, I used to pretend to be him to get around the castle sometimes. He never minded hanging back with his books while the three of us went exploring. Though *he never minded, I was always so grateful to him for letting me be him on those days; they were the only times I got to be a normal kid. Even his dad would play along." He chucked sadly.*

My brow knit as I listened. It was clear he still cared deeply for the boys he had grown up with.

"Callum and Logan, much like Asher and I, looked a lot alike. Both with blond hair and light eyes." He trailed off. "They were often mistaken for twins." He flexed his jaw, hand gripping his stomach as some kind of phantom pain drifted over his features. "I had not seen either of them for one hundred years, and I only saw the profile of my attacker... golden hair, light eyes. I knew instantly that it was one of them, but in my delirium, I could not tell who." His fist clenched as if he was angry he could not pinpoint which one of his friends had hurt him.

"I'm so sorry." I gripped his hand in a way I hoped he would find comforting. "From what you said, at least we can be sure it's not Asher," I offered.

"I can't be sure of anything," he said grimly.

"Well, Callum saved us both back there and saved me from being sold into slavery, so that puts him in the trusted category to me."

"I would have never let them take you, I would have died trying to protect you."

White-hot anger churned in my stomach. "But you shouldn't put yourself at risk like that for me."

"Why not?" He glared, voice low.

"You have to save the world!"

"I can't become human without you. I can't do any of this without you, it would be pointless."

"Well, not to me. I'm sure the king has some kind of

backup plan. Even if you can't be human again, you could still fight Skithian."

"You have too much faith in me."

"You kept fighting even after you were hurt. You could have died, but you care about your people, about your kingdom, so you fought," I said, trying to put my heart back in its place. I was one of his subjects. I had the king's power. He would have fought for anyone in my position.

"I fought—" He stopped, looking flustered. "I should have fought harder, so that man would have never had a chance to lay a finger on you, let alone..." He bit down hard, his jaw clicking.

I frowned, not wanting to think about that man's mouth on mine. Shame rolled over me, not just about what the horrible man had done, but how I too had forced myself on Shroding in the beginning, not understanding he was a real person. It wasn't quite the same, but it was similar in some ways.

"I'm so sorry, I don't think I ever apologized to you for kissing you all that time ago."

"What?" He grimaced, eyes flashing. "You mean to tell me the shame you are feeling is because of the kiss we shared and not from that monster?"

I flinched at his words. Had he thought I was a monster when I kissed him? Was that why he was so angry?

I jumped when he grabbed my shoulders and forced me to face him.

"I wasn't angry because of the reason you think. I have never once thought of you as a monster." He sounded so firm and yet so broken, like he was hurting too. "Our kiss was nothing like what happened between you and—" He broke off, rage causing him to shake.

I chewed my lip in fear. Over and over in my head I said to him I was sorry, so very sorry. I deserved his anger.

"Enough!" he bit out. "There is nothing to forgive." He let me go, fist clenching as if he wanted to strike something. "Strings, I should be apologizing to you for not protecting you better, but you're apologizing to me..." He lifted his gaze, dark eyes heavy with the many years he had lived. "They are not the same thing. You didn't want to kiss him."

I was about to protest that Shroding hadn't wanted to kiss me either, but he continued, "It's not that I didn't want to kiss you then, it's just that there was so much you didn't understand, and it didn't seem right. I was confused." His shoulders dropped as he scratched the back of his neck. "I mean, I was thirteen when I became a cat, I hadn't—"

I blinked. His words and the blush that completely covered his neck and cheeks scrambled in my mind to make sense. He. Had. Wanted. To. Kiss. Me? He had wanted to, but was afraid he wouldn't be any good at it? Had it been his first kiss? No, that couldn't be right. His desire to kiss me was probably because he was curious about the emotions.

I laughed a little. "Regardless, I shouldn't have done it, not like that," I asserted because I did want to kiss him again, because I wanted to know if it could be as electric as it had been the first time and because I was coming to love Shroding in a way I had not truly thought possible in such a short amount of time.

"Tell me you understand that our kiss and what happened to you are completely different?"

"I understand." I nodded.

He looked relieved and swallowed. "I'm so sorry that happened to you."

"Me too." I shivered, letting him encase me in his arms, pulling me close.

When I had stopped shaking, he pulled back and gave me a crooked smile.

"I vow the next time you are kissed, it will be because you want it."

Did he know that the next kiss I wanted to have was from him?

"Same for you," I promised. It was the least I could do, because even if it was not me who got to kiss him next, I wanted to make sure it was someone he really wanted.

He chuckled. "Now, to be sure that nothing like that ever happens again, we ought to do a bit of training, what do you think?"

"Sounds like a plan to me."

CHAPTER 14
Sledding

The far-off rumble of another storm was a reminder of the ground we had already covered. We had left the shelter of the tree two days prior. We covered a lot of ground, and despite the difficulty, Shroding had not let us fail. He kept us moving forward with a determination to get us through the "most dangerous" part of the mountain, as he had called it.

Cold air shot through the threads of my sweater, numbing the skin beneath. I kept Callum's blanket tight around me but longed for the warm coat Shroding had gotten me. I had managed most nights because Shroding never let the fire go out, but I would freeze if we did not find another shelter soon. We were getting better at transferring the king's power to make fires, and I had most of the basic Krav forms memorized even though I was not very good at performing them. The food from Callum's pack was nearly gone, thanks to our delay.

Howls in the wind made the hairs on my neck stand on end, but we kept our small party moving, not stopping, not even slowing. We had drawn the attention of a pack of wolves, who had been stalking us for the last hour or so. Etienne was getting skittish with every howl, and just when the last one sounded close beside us, I asked Shroding, "What should we do? They're not stopping."

"We have to keep moving." His pace quickened, the only sign that he too was nervous.

A snarl sounded to my left, and before I knew what was happening, Etienne whinnied as one of the beasts lunged from the trees, its hungry eyes locking with mine as it cut off our escape.

The pack charged us, scratching Etienne's underbelly, breaking the saddle strap, sending me flying. I hit the ground, and a snapping reverberated through my body. I screamed. Something hot and wet slid down my neck, and I rolled over to throw up. My vision speckled, confusion overtaking me. How had I ended up on the ground? My ears rang as I tried to sit up, my movements sluggish and vision blurred. A growl came close to my head, and I flinched.

"Haya!" Shroding yelled.

Leaves and twigs cracked; claws dragged through the dirt near my legs, and I shuffled back. I struggled to breath through the nausea. My vision blackened, and I lay down as the tussle and growls continued to clatter around me.

Galloping hooves moved further and further away.

"Haya, Haya, can you hear me? Please. Wake up." Something rough—sandpaper?—no, Shroding's tongue rubbed my fingers. I opened my eyes, not sure when they had closed. Shroding was at my side.

He made a strange whimpered meow, a sound I had never heard before. I smiled weakly. My shoulder sparked with pain, and I grimaced. Wetness caked the side of my face and neck. My left calf was exposed to the cold air. I was definitely bleeding. I used a nearby tree to help me sit up and leaned back with my good arm.

"I'm okay." I took in my appearance. "Ish."

He said nothing and just watched me. I could tell he was trying hard not to let me hear his thoughts. The first beams of light I'd seen in days feathered down through the trees.

I looked around the clearing. How had the attack ended so fast? "Etienne is gone?" I frowned.

"The wolves followed the bigger meal, finding us too much of a fight."

I didn't feel like much of a fight. I was easy food, but I supposed Shroding had done enough to scare them away as he had done with the soldiers and marauders before.

"Was he injured?" I asked, worried for Micah's horse.

"No, he was unharmed when he ran away."

"Well, at least there's that." I sighed.

My last piece of home had just left me. I really had nothing of my old life now. In the back of my mind, I had thought Etienne might be the one thing that could bring me home. I think I had hoped he would give me a reason to go back to Wycliff someday, to return him to Micah. Now that reason was gone. Bile, hot and sour, burned my throat. I turned my head to throw up but only dry heaved a horrible sob, and I wasn't sure if it was from emotional or physical pain.

"Can you walk?" Shroding asked, his voice strained. Why had the wolves chased Etienne when I was down on the ground, easy prey?

"I can try." I attempted to stand, careful of my arm. My calf had a deep gash, and I awkwardly used the tree I leaned on for support.

"Why did the wolves leave me? I should be wolf supper by now." I tried to joke, though the searing pain in my arm and leg made it sound sharp instead of playful. "Don't get me wrong," I continued. "I'm really glad to be alive."

"Perhaps they had something else to be afraid of," Shroding grumbled darkly. My eyes widened in surprise as I took in four wolves that lay a few feet away unmoving.

"Strap this around me." I looked over. Shroding nudging the saddle with his nose, flipping it over so it was upside down.

"Why?" My voice was small. Had he killed four wolves, alone? Even after fighting the marauders' dogs and getting injured? How in the world had he managed that?

"I can pull you," he said simply.

"I'm too heavy," I protested.

"I can pull you," he asserted, his voice chilling.

"But—"

"The buckle is useless, you will have to tie it," he continued, ignoring me.

I knelt and attempted to strap him in with my one good arm. "This isn't working," I groaned as my hand slipped again.

"Tie it first, and then I'll step into it." His voice was even colder, and I struggled not to take offense at his directness.

I took a breath and used my good foot and hand to tie a knot at the end. He stepped into the loop, and I crossed the straps on his chest, over and under his back and belly. He was covered in blood, but I could not tell if it was his or that of the beasts he had taken down.

"It worked," I said, surprised.

"Sit," he ordered, and I could tell he was trying very hard

not to sound choleric. "I will pull us to the palace, it's not much further."

I nodded and sat on the underside of the saddle.

He pulled me with ease.

"How are you able to–?" I trailed off. Together the saddle and I had to weigh close to two hundred pounds.

"Even though I am a cat, I still have the muscle mass of a human," he said as he pulled. He moved slowly but moved nonetheless.

"Wouldn't that make you huge?"

"Think of it this way—I am dense." He explained. "I have the strength of a full-grown man compacted into the muscles of a larger than average cat."

"So that would make you really heavy?" I panted, trying to keep talking. I could tell I was going to pass out again. If I had a concussion, which I was pretty sure I did, I could not go to sleep. Father had taught me the signs, just as he had told me the signs of shock. It was like he'd been preparing me for this journey, and maybe he had been. No. That was probably the concussion talking. I forced myself to stay awake, shaking my head slightly. The movement made my stomach roll.

"Yes, that is why I never let you pick me up and why I never sat on you like a normal cat would." I nodded my understanding but regretted the movement as my vision swam. "One, I'm too big, and two, I would have probably crushed you had I put my full weight on you."

I winced at the word "crushed," feeling my shoulder throb. I didn't think it was broken, but it sure radiated pain like it was.

"So that's how you were able to fight the wolves, the marauders' dogs, and the soldiers back in Wycliff?" I reasoned, finally putting together how he could take down fully grown men.

"Yes, I'm a lot stronger than I seem. It has its advantages." He was breathing heavily.

"Indeed," I said lightly, gesturing to the makeshift sled.

"Put pressure on your leg to try to stop the bleeding," he said, peering back at me.

"Right." I nodded, pulling my leg towards me with some effort. I looked around my body for anything to wrap my leg with. My braid curved over my shoulder, the light green ribbon catching my eye. It had been in the pocket of the coat Shroding had given me. Probably a gift a father was going to give his daughter. I thought of my own father and imagined him giving me this pretty green fabric to tie my hair back with. I imagined having a pretty green dress to match. The way my eyes would pop a more vibrant green. The lightness and freedom the picture painted in me were quickly replaced with the image of my blood-coated pants. The muddy color of my blonde hair. With remorse and bitterness, I untied the ribbon, which I had wrapped over the cord holding my hair. Slowly I twisted it around my calf and clamped my good hand over top and pressed.

We rounded a ridge, the weight of the saddle crushing the cold earth. Despite my efforts to stay awake, I drifted in and out of consciousness, too weak to move dimensions.

Every once in a while I could hear Shroding checking to see if I was okay, but he never stopped moving, never stopped pulling, even when he growled and hissed with the effort.

The sun was low when I woke next, Shroding's sweet voice coaxing me.

"There is a small house up ahead."

I forced my eyes open and tried to see what he did, but couldn't. My vision was not nearly as sharp as his cat senses.

He glanced at my leg, which I had given up putting pressure on, the pretty green ribbon a deep, morbid crimson. "You need treatment now."

I turned and could faintly see the small house, lights brightening its two front windows. It was not ideal that someone was home, but what choice did we have. I nodded, and we dipped into the valley, breaking the tree line. A long brown fence stretched out before us, surrounding the cabin.

"Ugh!" Shroding groaned as the strap broke on his side. The saddle recoiled with the motion, and I rolled, my body tensing as I flopped to the ground, thankfully landing on my good shoulder. Shroding was at my side, the straps hanging limply across his back and dragging in the dirt. He pushed dirt from my face with his furry cheek.

"Just go, get help. I'll be okay." I moaned, sitting up. Wolves howled in the distance, and I flinched. Had they gotten Etienne and were circling back to us, or had Etienne proven too hard to catch? Or was it a different pack altogether following our trail of blood? I closed my eyes, trying to will the panic away.

"I will not leave you unless I know it is safe. Right now it's not," he said roughly. "If I had arms, I would just carry you," he clipped, unable to mask his frustration.

For a moment, guilt swelled within me. I kept falling apart in front of him, getting hurt and sick. Shroding had not said it to make me feel bad. I could tell he was aggravated with himself for putting me in more trouble, but I still felt responsible.

"Can you walk? Just to the house? Just a little bit

further?" he encouraged, lifting my good arm over his back as leverage to help me stand.

I swallowed and clutched his fur tightly as I put all my weight on him, shuffling my feet under me. Gritting my teeth with the effort, I held in the cry that wanted to escape. I would not show how much pain I was in. I would push through. I was pushing through a lot of emotional pain lately, and it was as if this physical pain was an outward expression of everything inside. Even with blood exposed, I was still trying to hide that pain.

I masked it poorly, because Shroding knew exactly how much I was struggling both emotionally and physically.

Still I persevered forward in slow, measured steps. We were both silent, concentrating on getting to the house above anything else.

We made our way up the steps of the white wood porch. I gripped the railing, sure I would fall at any moment.

"Someone's inside," Shroding warned, but we already knew as much.

I grunted, unable to say anything else. Everything hurt so much, the pain mind numbing.

"We have to take this risk," Shroding said, more to himself than to me. I understood his hesitation. We did not know what would be on the other side of this door, or if they would be able to feel the king's power. If this would draw the Wraiths to our location and cost another person their home or life.

I knocked on the door.

"Miles!" a small elderly white-haired woman cried while opening the door. Her face was wide with a smile. "Oh!" she gasped, and quickly tried to close the door, her smile falling.

I could not fault her, our appearances were no doubt terrifying.

"Ma'am, please can you help me? I was thrown from my horse and need medical attention." I gestured to my leg as I gripped the railing again, unsteady on my feet.

"Oh dear! Oh dear!" She looked around, seeing I was alone. "Come in, dear. It's so late, why are you wandering out alone?" The lady had deep wrinkles around her eyes, and a slight hunch in her back. She gestured for me to come in, and I limped after her. She pulled out a chair for me to sit on, and I gratefully collapsed into it, needing no other invitation. The room was small, with the kitchen open to the right and three doors, bedrooms I assumed, to the left. "Sit, sit," she repeated, even though I was already sitting. "I will get the medical kit." She walked off into one of the rooms.

Shroding came to sit at my side.

"See? Nothing bad." I smiled, though I was still a little nervous. Could this lady really help me?

"Hmm," Shroding answered, eyes scanning the rather sparse room.

"Dear me, your poor leg. Oh, and that arm!" She came back, taking a long look at my appearance, a box of medication in her hand. "It's a good thing I was a nurse in Erasmus in my youth. I'll get you patched up!"

I stiffened, not sure when I had started to relax, and glanced at Shroding. She had been to Erasmus, so she was familiar with the front lines, which meant she might be able to sense vibration abilities. I shifted in the chair, unsure what to do.

Her white-lashed eyes followed my gaze. "Your cat?" she asked, tilting her head to look at Shroding.

"Um, yes."

"He is very... unique."

"Um, yes, he is." My whole body tightened at our exchange, ready to run from the small house, but Shroding seemed to relax, lying down at the foot of my chair.

I took this as a sign she wasn't dangerous. He would know if she could sense vibrations better than I would. It wasn't second nature to me yet, as I still had much to learn.

The lady shook her head and tended to my leg first. She cleaned the deep gash, which I was sure would scar. When she began to stitch it, I nearly passed out again. The room spun with the pain, and I gripped the edges of the chair to keep from falling. Sweat poured down my neck as I held back my cries of pain.

Once she was done, she moved her attention to my arm. "Take that sweater off, dear, and come sit closer to the fire."

Awkwardly I scooted my chair closer to the hearth but hesitated to strip my sweater. I peered at Shroding, whose head was turned away from us. It was nothing he hadn't seen before, I supposed. So with some effort I lifted my shirt over my head, until, unsurprisingly, it got stuck on my injured arm, and the lady had to help me get it off the rest of the way. I smiled at her, grateful for her gentleness.

Meticulously she poked around my shoulder and down my arm. "Well," she said with a small smile, "good news is it's not broken, but you will have a very nasty bruise for a while. Lots of scar tissue, which will hurt."

"Not broken?" I sighed. I'd known it wasn't, but why did it feel like it was? "Are you sure? It feels very, very broken." I winced.

"It will hurt severely for a few days. It's dislocated. I'll just pop it back in," she said, and without any more warning, she snapped my shoulder back in place. All the pain I had suppressed came out in one short earsplitting scream that seemed to echo in the cabin.

"Oh, calm down. You are lucky—a fall from a horse should have broken something. Perhaps your head," she said jokingly. I gave a dismayed laugh, adrenaline making me more alert than I had in days. "Hmm, it looks like you have a concussion," she noted, staring deeply into my eyes, making me uncomfortable. "Your pupils are not dilated, so it is safe for you to sleep."

I glanced at Shroding, embarrassed. The grandma seemed nice enough, if a little weird, and I was grateful for her assessment of my injuries, but was it really safe to stay here any longer?

"Thank you." I shifted, my lips twitching my thanks.

"Well, dear, you are as patched up as I can manage. Go wash, you're covered in blood. I will try to find some suitable clothes."

A shower? A hot shower. I would have hugged the old lady if not for my shoulder. "Oh, thank you so much, ma'am..." I started to stand, but hesitated. I took in the small table in the kitchen where she had pulled the chair from. It was set with all kinds of vegetables, potatoes and meats. "Before," I began, "when you opened the door you called for someone named Miles?"

"Yes, yes, my eldest son. He is coming home today. He was supposed to be home an hour ago. I prepared a whole meal for him." She gestured to where I was looking. "Since you're here, it won't go to waste."

My mind drifted to the bag of provisions that had rode away with Etienne. "I could not possibly impose so much!" I wobbled on my good leg, hunger making me nearly fling myself at the table.

"No, no, please wash up and come eat." She pointed to the middle of the three doors; a bathroom.

My mouth watered, but I walked into the washroom first.

"Well, kitty, you need some medical attention now too."

I paused leaning against the inside of the bathroom door, I listened to the elderly woman coo at Shroding. He was hurt? He had said nothing. I had been too preoccupied with my own injuries to notice his.

"Roll on to your side, please, so I can see how far that cut goes."

I swallowed. When he had gotten hurt? Was it from carrying me? Was it from the wolves? I waited till it sounded like he was all patched up before I closed the door to the bathroom.

The room was small, like everything in the house, but clean. Pale pink tiles lined the floor and the shower walls. I turned on the hot water and stripped away my tattered and muddy clothes. The circular mirror fogged up with the steam, but I could still make out my thin tired face. My green eyes were dull in the dim light of the bathroom.

I let the hot water pour down my skin, leaving it splotchy and red. I scrubbed my scalp and body as aggressively as I could with one hand. I tried not to play back the events of the day. I was about to climb out when the bathroom door opened, and I froze. I pressed firmly against the wall, my body blocked from view by a tiled divider.

"I've put some towels and clean clothes on the counter here. They might be a little big but will do. Also your cat could use a rinse." When I didn't respond, she left, the door closing behind her. I gasped, realizing I had been holding my breath. I peered around the corner. The clothes lay on the counter just as she'd said.

"Haya," Shroding said from the spot on the floor by my pile of dirty clothes. I blinked at the sight of him.

"What are you doing here?" I snapped, pressing again as far back as I could go, the divider feeling far too small.

"She insisted I get washed. She was going to pick me up, so I ran inside before she could." He sounded embarrassed, apologetic and something else that made my cheeks hot.

"Well, um, I'm not exactly dressed," I whispered, peering around the divider.

"Are you finished?"

I nodded.

"Then I'll close my eyes. You come out, and I'll go in and sit under the water for a while." He sounded so tired, and before I could respond, he closed his eyes, waiting. So I stepped out of the shower, wrapping my body in a towel.

"Okay," I whispered. His eyes opened, but he did not look my way. He walked straight into the shower and under the spray. The water hit his back, turning brown and red as it poured down the drain. He looked miserable, and I could tell he wasn't going to get clean just sitting there.

I secured the towel around my body, and took the showerhead down by the long cord. The water was warm as I brought the nozzle close to his fur.

His eyes flew open and stared wide-eyed at me. "W-What are you doing?"

"Let me help," I said gently. It was not the first time I had washed him. The very first night we met, he had followed me inside the house, covered in fleas, and not knowing who he was, I had bathed him. Now it was different, because I knew he was a man, though he looked like a cat.

He said nothing, just observed me with his dark eyes as I meticulously glided the nozzle over his fur. And as the water took away the dirt and blood, I could begin to see all the damage he had taken. Teeth marks littered his shoulders; the burns from the fire at the farmhouse were still raised and puckered; then there were the patches of missing fur from his back legs, where gnarled gashes cut through his skin. The elderly woman had stitched the worst of them.

I tapped his back legs, signaling him to stand up, and he did. I took a little soap and rubbed it along his back, moving out to his tail and feet. We were silent the whole time, a tension in the air I could not ignore. Though I was not sure if it was anger and offense that I was bathing him or perhaps enjoyment. A wild side of me hoped for the latter.

I rubbed the soap onto his head, his purring putting me in a state of ease. Maybe it was the hot water, the feeling of being clean, the feeling of being somewhere even just a little bit safe, or the sound of his purring that made everything from the last few days seem distant, almost bearable. I sighed, my eyes feeling heavy. His eyes were closed. Had he fallen asleep? Gently I nudged him to lie on his side, but he did not move, so I slid the nozzle under his belly to rinse there. He winced, eyes opening to glare at me, and moved away from the spray. My heart squeezed in my chest, but I beckoned him to me and lowered the water pressure so it was nothing more than a dribble. Cautiously I began to clean his stomach. The swirl of red trailing to the drain made panic well up in me.

"It's not as bad as it looks," he said softly, though pain laced his tone. The water must be burning the cut; as it had burned on my leg as I showered. I traced along the stitching. The cut ran from his chest to his back right hip. I recalled how the strap had wrapped around him and guilt gnawed at me. When the water ran mostly clear, I flipped off the tap.

"Okay." I grabbed a towel off the counter. I wrung out his fluffy tail and squeezed the extra water from his paws.

"Thanks, I'll take it from here," he said, moving past me out of the shower.

"Wait." I turned, wrapping the towel around his legs and torso till he was just a head and tail. "Can't have you catching a kitty cold," I teased, standing up, blood rushing to my legs at the movement. He glowered at me, the wet fur on his head standing up in crazy directions. I tried not to laugh, and I found a brush to comb out my hair, not caring that I was in just a towel before the future king of Shamar. I braided my hair down my back and dug around in the drawers till I found a new cord to tie it with, as mine was covered in grime and blood. I peered over at Shroding, who had burrowed in the towel, his eyes closed. Was he asleep?

Taking the opportunity, I looked over the clothes. They were big. A large cream linen shirt and waist-tie black pants that pooled around my feet. I was grateful for the bra, though it was a bit too small, and thick wool socks to stave off the cold.

I paused, glancing at Shroding. He was definitely unconscious. I took the opportunity to brush his tail and head, a small clump of fur coming off in the bristles. His silver fur twisted between the teeth, and I plucked the tuft out, sticking it into my pocket. After rolling up the pant legs twice, I was ready to go out and see the old lady again.

"Now that's better, right? How's the leg?" She smiled, sitting at the table.

"Good, I wrapped it before getting dressed," I affirmed, as she had left bandages next to the clothes for me.

"Good, dear. Now come sit and eat."

I did. We ate, and she told me about her time on the front

lines. Many of her stories were similar to the ones my father had shared, and though it made me a little sad, I listened with a reverence I hadn't before. My father was gone, but stories like his continued on, and something about this, about those shared experiences, removed some of my sadness.

After I had eaten enough for two, I found my eyes closing.

"Dear me, you must be exhausted. You can rest in my son's room."

"Thank you so much, you have no idea how grateful I am," I gushed sleepily.

"You are a dear thing. Are you on your way to Tyndale?"

I hesitated, not sure if Shroding would want me to answer honestly or not. "In that direction, yes," I said vaguely.

"Well, I'll pack you up some food and water for the journey, it's at least half a day by horse."

"I don't have a horse anymore, it ran off after throwing me."

"I have an old girl like me in the fields. Please take her."

"I can't possibly," I stressed, waving my hands.

"Now don't go saying things like that. You will have to bring her back, of course. I still have to introduce you to my son. He will like you, such a pretty girl." She grinned, a twinkle in her eyes.

I blushed. Was she trying to set me up?

"Oh, well, of course I'll return your horse," I agreed awkwardly, not wanting, at all, to meet her son.

She got me settled in the bedroom. Would Shroding be okay in the bathroom? He had been breathing when I left, so there wasn't really a reason to worry? Was there?

"The sheets are clean, go ahead and get some sleep. I'll

wake you when the sun is high." She left the door open a crack and went to clean up the kitchen. I wanted to offer help, but didn't have the energy. Instead I crawled under the quilt and was soon drifting.

"Oh, you're awake." The faint whisper of the old lady filled my half-asleep mind. "I guess I should feed you too," she said, but I could not see who she was talking to.

Shroding gave a distinct meow, and I fell asleep wondering for a moment where he'd learned to meow like that.

Just like a cute house cat.

CHAPTER 15

Why Didn't You Save Him?

POCKET DIMENSION

I sat in the valley where the cabin was and called for Shroding.

He settled down in the grass next to me, the mountains cresting up infront of us. Before I could question him, mostly to ask how he was feeling and grill him as to why he hadn't told me he was injured, he spoke.

"I know there are a lot of things you want to know about me and everything we are facing." He hedged, "Don't take this the wrong way, but I have some questions about you too."

"Oh?" Absently, I picked a leaf off the ground and rolled it between my fingers. "Like what?"

"Your family, your friends... those kids on the farm everyday."

I glanced at him, which was a mistake. His eyes flickered iridescent, and my cheeks flushed as I recalled the night he had carried me out of the barn in the other dimension. The otherworldly glow around him had seemed so fanciful then.

Now I knew that was just who he was, a magnet to the light. I was a girl floundering around in the dark, shrouded by night, but he was the sky full of stars, helping me find my way. "What specifically do you want to know?"

"Your mother, what is she like?" he asked, and I couldn't help but wonder if his asking was because he'd lacked the presence of his own mother growing up. I imagined Queen Elina would have been a wonderful mother, loving, attentive, and even with her prophecy telling of the power her son would have, I bet it wouldn't have mattered one bit to her.

"She looks like me, but her hair is shorter and her face is covered in freckles, making her seem young. Anytime we were in town together, visiting vendors, they would always tease us, saying we looked more like sisters." I grinned at the memory. "Everyone loves her, she is hard working, and somehow even when my father was away for business, she always kept the plates spinning. Never letting the farm fall behind. She is my hero in more ways than one." I sighed, an ache in my chest yawning open. I missed her so much. I wrapped my arms around myself, hugging tightly. My long hair tumbled over my shoulder, and I shrugged it back with a tilt of my head. "I was notorious for getting things caught in my hair." I chuckled without humor. "On the day she left, it had gotten caught on the button of her coat sleeve." I swallowed thickly.

"She sounds incredibly strong." Shroding gave a comforting smile. "You take after her in more than looks."

I waved away the compliment. I hadn't been able to do half of what she could do. I had more than failed the farm; I'd let it burn.

Shroding placed a hand on my shoulder, clearing his throat. "What is her name, you didn't say?"

"Jean Golden, and then there is Theo," I added, the smile that had been forming falling just as quickly into a frown.

He shifted, hands folding in his lap as silence descended between us.

I knew I needed to talk about them, to work through the grief, but it was harder than I'd ever thought possible.

"Haya ...I know what it's like to lose the people you love... It does get easier even if it never quite goes away."

It was true, he did understand, but his losses were over two hundred years ago; mine were a few days ago. But perhaps the hope he offered held some truth. If he had continued to live on even after losing his parents and being turned into a cat, isolated and alone, then I too would overcome in time. He had no one, but I had him, and that was a lot.

After a few moments I whispered, "What else did you want to know?"

"The kids?"

"They are orphans and children of widows. We do what we can to keep them financially afloat. At least, we did. I don't know what they will do now... without the farm."

Shroding didn't seem to know what to say to that but after a moment continued his questions. "Do you have any friends? You seemed relatively alone on the farm."

"I have a pen pal. She lives in Romath, though." I hesitated. "Then there's Micah."

Shroding's folded hands tightened, the golden skin of his fingers paling to almost white. "Yes, Micah. Can you tell me about him?"

My throat constricted as I thought about our last moments together. How he had let me go with such hope in his eyes. Had he really loved me? Had he proposed because of his promise to his father? To keep our family safe? What better way than to *marry me, even though we were so young. Most people got married after they finished the mandatory service, but even those without the gift waited till at least their twenties. But my father always said war changes things: how we love, when we love and the way we love. Still, in our little town the war had seemed so far away, like it would never reach us. Until it did. Until Theo and father had left. Until just a few days ago when my childhood burned down, and the only safety net I thought I had left, snapped.*

Shroding and Micah were nothing alike, and not just because Shroding was a cat and a prince, but because I had always believed Micah to be transparent. He asked for what he wanted and was direct about his expectations. He thought the best about everyone and always encouraged me to trust people. In the end, though, he had not trusted me, and I supposed I would never know for sure if his proposal was out of love or obligation.

Shroding had done just the opposite. I'd hesitated to trust him, and he'd waited for me to come to him, to draw my own conclusions about who he was. He was honest, painfully so, and constantly reminded me that I knew nothing about his world and what it was like. His world was complicated and contradictory. Danger and hope warring at every twist and turn. Yet, I had no doubt about his character. He was patient and kind. Persistent and strong. He had a quality about him that made you want to follow. Maybe that was just his kingly nature or the way he made you choose him without even asking to be chosen. But all of it resonated true, in a way that nothing in my life had before. He was just a man with an extraordinary mission, and he bore it with a grace I was humbled by and thankful for.

"Haya?" Shroding touched my arm softly.

"I'm sorry. I don't think I can do this yet." I wanted to tell him, talk to him, open the wound and share its pain with someone, but was still uncertain. Not of the prince but of myself. What could I offer the prince beside the king's power and the dismal remains of the girl I once was? Again the question nagged at me. Who was I without the people who raised me, loved me and taught me? I didn't know, and without knowing that, I didn't feel certain of anything.

"I understand..." He hesitated. "Can I ask you just one more thing?"

I nodded.

"What was your father's name?"

I returned my attention to the leaf I had been twisting; hearing my father talked about in the past tense sobered me like ice water being dumped over my head. It was almost enough to silence me from talking altogether.

"Armond Golden," I whispered. "He was named after my..." I turned to look at Shroding, something Micah had said coming together in my mind.

Shroding's brows knit.

"What is it?" I asked instead.

"That was the name of the general." Shroding pushed up the sleeves of his cream tunic, the color making his tanned skin appear richer, and the motion drawing attention to his veined forearms. "The general for my father, the one at the palace the night I was transformed into a cat."

"My father was named after one of my ancestors." I nodded. "Micah said my very great-grandfather knew the king. Your father must have given the king's power to him, and somehow it passed down each generation till it got to me." I gasped, covering my mouth.

Shroding raised a dark brow at me.

"'What was needed is passed down,' just like the king's journal said," I explained.

He ran his fingers through his hair, the pensive look on his face making me slightly anxious. "Guess that's it, then," he agreed. Still, the look of other grim musings was evident in his dark eyes, but my own thoughts distracted me from drawing them out.

If the power was passed down, did that mean it had passed to Theo?

My father had waited eagerly to see which one of us would get the gift. When Theo finally did, Father had been so relieved. So did that mean the gift Theo had was the king's power? And when he died, was that when the power passed to me? Was that why I'd suddenly gone from not having the gift to having it?

The dream of us as kids filled my mind, the warning Theo had given me, saying, "I'm afraid this burden will pass to you now." Theo had known and somehow cautioned me of what was to come, but if that was true, then Shroding should have been able to talk to Theo, just as he was talking to me now. Shroding could have saved him. So why hadn't he?

The air became thin; the realization was too much like standing on the edge of a cliff, waiting to see if I would fall.

"What is it?" Shroding turned the full force of his onyx eyes on me, no doubt feeling the burst of horror and dread emanating from every cell in my body.

I stared back, determined to get an answer even if it hurt.

"Why didn't you help him?"

His brow furrowed, and he looked taken aback. "Who—?" Then, as I feared it might, understanding lit in his eyes. "Theo?"

"Yes," I whispered with barely a sound.

"Because..." His words were steady, but his gaze dropped to the grass as his feet. "... he did not ask me to."

I flinched as if he'd struck me. "What do you mean?" My voice rose. "I know Theo had nightmares, they plagued him for months. He was moving dimensions in his sleep too? Wasn't he?!" I demanded, but I didn't let him get a word in. "Theo was horribly sick. He could not sleep or eat." Like I had been for weeks, except Theo had been that way for months.

"Theo struggled because I was not there to help him. He did not call for me when he moved to the rip, when he faced the Wraiths, like you did."

"I don't understand. Why couldn't you just go to him! I didn't know I needed to call for you till you told me to. How did you not know he needed you?" I stressed, falling to my knees in front of the prince, wishing I could understand how he could abandon my brother. "How could you not know that I needed you to save him?" My voice broke because of course he would not have known that. At the time Shroding hadn't known who I was, and though it was not Shroding's fault, in some ways blaming him was easier than understanding his perspective. My brother hadn't needed to suffer, he hadn't needed to die.

"I only knew you were hurting because I was so close to you in the physical world, because as Iri I was there next to you as you wrestled in your sleep. And I only knew I had to be called after I saw the pattern with you. When you called for help the first two times, I showed up without you calling for me by name."

"Then he never called for help?" I demanded, barely listening to his reasons.

"He did once. I remember it very clearly. I had tried to tell him the truth. Everything I have only just exposed fully to you in the last few days, but he didn't believe me." He ran his fingers through his hair roughly as if this was not the first time he had labored over these events. "I didn't know why I appeared to him, I didn't know he had to call for help. I didn't know how any of this worked." He sighed as if the weight of this confession caused him physical pain. "When I saw Theo, spoke to him, it was the first time I could interact with someone. The first time in two hundred years." His dark eyes glistened with tears as they met mine. "Haya, I was... overwhelmed." He turned his head to the side, dragging his hand over his eyes. "It's not an excuse... Despite how I felt, he didn't want my help, because he never called for it again."

Shroding's tears were like a blunt dagger to my sternum, the pain that had been growing there overshadowed by his remorse. He had taken my accusations in stride, not raising his voice once in response. He was calm, the echo of sorrow permeating every single one of his words. Sorrow that matched mine. He would have helped Theo, as he had helped me, if Theo had given him the chance. Shame over my outburst rolled through me. I could not fault him for what he had not known.

I collapsed to the ground next to Shroding's bent knee. "You spoke to him?"

"We talked for a long time, but in the end Theo wanted no part of my story. He told me he would make his own path." Shroding shrugged, but even that gesture of nonchalance was blanketed in contrition. "He did not choose me, and I could not force him to believe me."

Theo, for all his good qualities, was stubborn. He was not an acceptor, he was a challenger. His choices were wholly his own. If he didn't want something, no one would have been able to change his mind. I think he had to be that way.

Growing up sick and weak, he could not accept his frailty lest it define him. He chose to fight back. A trait I had admired, but in the end his fighting spirit had led him to fight against the one thing that could have saved him.

"You said I was the first person you had spoken to in hundreds of years," I recalled, skeptical, as he had just admitted to talking to my brother first.

"Yes, well, I only spoke with him once, but I thought it was a fluke. I didn't have all the signs I had with you. At that time I did not fully understand how or why I had found him in this dimension. I was not near Wycliff. I was deep in these mountains." He looked up at the sky. "I was caught off guard just as much as he was." He sombered. "I didn't mean to keep it from you, but I did fear you finding out. I realized who he was to you after we met, after I was convinced you had the king's power. I worried that if you knew, you would choose your own path as he had. That I wouldn't be able to protect you. I just didn't want to tell you everything right away. I did that with Theo, and he ran from me. I hope you understand."

"How did Theo survive the nightmares... I nearly died from them."

"I can't say for sure. You mentioned he trained his gift and got stronger, right?"

"Yes, he joined the military with my father after he was better, but the nightmares had already ended by that point, or at least he stopped talking about them."

"Was there someone who could have trained him in secret? Your father, perhaps?"

"It's possible."

"I think he learned how to fight the Wraiths. He must have learned how to use the king's power."

"Like how I am learning to fight?"

He nodded.

I took in his fear and concern, believing he meant every word, because if I had been in his place, I would have feared the same things. I understood him, and that made me very different from my brother. Still, I did not like things being kept from me.

"There is nothing else? Nothing else you are withholding?"

But before he could answer, I was startled awake by yelling.

CHAPTER 16

Dangerous Allies

"Mother, can't you feel it? The powers coming from her?"

I started and blinked for a moment, forgetting where I was.

"Miles, calm down. She is harmless."

The door of the room burst open, and a tall young man came in, his hair dark, unkempt and crazy in the dim light peeking through the closed curtains.

I bolted upright, the room shaking like the night when the Grieving attacked the farmhouse. My eyes locked with the young man.

"What—" I tried to speak, but was roughly pushed back, pinned by my shoulders to the headboard. I cried out as the pain in my injured shoulder flared. Vibrations, wild and roiling, slammed into my chest, crushing into me so forcefully, the wood of the headboard split against my back. My lungs were unable to expand for a full breath. I sputtered, desperate to understand what was happening.

Around his neck hung an odd-shaped black piece of

wood. It was so out of place with the rest of his clothes, which were all white and flowing, like something worn for a party or ceremony.

"Miles, please let the girl go!" The elderly woman begged from the doorway. She must have been sleeping, for she wore a gown and nightcap. So this was her son, the one she had been waiting for? I tried to look at him, but my eyes were growing unfocused.

"Who are you? Why are you here?" In a blur of movement that was very unnatural, Miles climbed over top of me. "Whose side are you on?" he demanded, his breath hot and sour against my face. With his face inches from mine, there was no hiding the pallor of his skin, the deranged look in his eyes, nor the wooden mask that displayed three white dots under the eyehole, hanging from his neck.

He was one of the marauders! Was he with the two men who'd attacked us? Had he followed us? More than that, unlike the other two, it was clear Miles had the vibration gift and had been using it on himself. He wasn't Grieving, not a walking corpse yet, but he was well on his way there, if the sunken look of his eyes was any warning of the vibration sickness.

I shook my head, grabbing Miles's arms to push him back. Why was he hurting me? Wasn't he from Shamar? It was forbidden for anyone in Shamar to use the gift in such a way. It was a disgrace. Shamar was far too proud and honorable to stoop to Golan's ways, or at least that was what I had always believed.

Shroding slammed his body into the side of the man, knocking him off me. The crunch of bones echoed in the small room.

"Haya, we need to leave now!" Shroding hissed as his body tumbled and slid to the door.

"Oh, Miles!" the lady cooed, lifting her son from the floor.

Air had only just filled my chest before Miles, shoving his mother off him, was stalking towards me again. The lady stumbled back, hitting the wall and crumpling to the floor, her brittle bones popping.

Anger pulsed through me, and without me trying, the king's power filled my tingling hands.

"Haya! Don't!" Shroding yelled, but I couldn't hear the rest of his words over the thunderous vibration, like a torrent inside me. Thousands of strings thrashed in me, spinning out of my control. A faint wisp of panic cautioned in the back of my mind as the gift burst through me, throwing Miles, before he could touch me, clean through the curtained windows and into the yard outside.

I gaped at my hands, breathing heavily, then looked at the older lady, who was unconscious by the doorway. Scrambling out of the bed, my whole body screaming with the effort it took to move, I begged her forgiveness, though she could not hear me.

"I-I am so, so sorry." I had destroyed another home, another family.

Horrified, I ran past her and out of the room. A bag leaned against the front doorframe, no doubt the bag she'd packed for us. I grabbed it and hurried outside, my feet bare as I followed Shroding back into the trees.

It was only when we were a good distance away that I registered my lack of coat, shoes, and the trail of warm blood seeping from the gash on my leg.

We hobbled through the forest in silence for a few hours; even with the sun overhead it was cold. Though we were a safe distance from the house, and the wolves were far behind us, Shroding was determined to keep us moving. He found a large stick I could put my weight on as we continued through the mountains. The ridges of his peaked shoulders remained tense as he walked on ahead.

We did not stop frequently, but when we did, it was to rewrap and rest my leg. I couldn't help but smile as he asked for what had to be the hundredth time how I was doing. His voice was full of worry and care for me.

"This is the halfway point." Shroding halted at the edge of a steep gully. "Or at least it would be if we were farther south, taking the path I originally planned, and we still had Etienne." He sighed heavily.

I knelt next to him.

"I suppose Callum was right about there being more than wild animals to contend with."

Shroding's dark eyes appraised me with what I could only imagine to be sarcasm as he said, "You're bleeding."

I patted my leg. "Too soon?" I teased, attempting to keep a straight face.

"We should cross," he deadpanned, looking between my leg and my face.

I laughed. A big, huge belly laugh at the ridiculous situation we were in. Despite the agony of my body, my heart was full and content. We had plenty of food and water, and even though the wolves and marauders had taken us off course, adding potentially days to our journey, I was not sad about it. Shroding had begun filling a gap I had not known could be full again. Theo and my father were gone, but in their place I'd been given someone who cared for me just as much. I had no doubt Shroding cared for me; I'm not sure I ever truly doubted him. The way he looked after me. The way he teased and encouraged me. The easy way we could talk. The only doubt came when I wondered how much he cared and why. I tried not to think about those questions, though; I had been cared for and even loved out of duty before. I never wanted to experience that again.

"Rest for now. I'll try to find an easy path across."

Needing no other prompting, I lay at the base of a pine, letting the warmth of the soft winter sun soothe the tension in my face. With our basic needs met, it was getting harder to distract my thoughts from my family, friends and the future. I closed my eyes. Had Etienne found his way home, back to Micah? Was Micah wondering about me? My thoughts ran to all those I had left behind to go on this journey. Talie, my pen pal, who I'd never sent the letter to. The children who would not have income to bring home to feed their families. My mother, who should have received my message by now. I could only hope she was safer than I was.

Before my mind could travel down darker thoughts, Shroding curled at my side.

"I think I found a spot you can get across."

I brushed my hands over his fur, massaging his ears. "Five more minutes," I muttered tiredly.

He purred, head nuzzling against my hand. We stayed that way for a while. Taking the stolen moment to let the fear and adrenaline of the morning fall off.

"How do we know when we have crossed into Tyndale?"

"When all you see ahead are rolling prairies perfect for rearing cattle." Shroding paused and added with a chuckle,

"But before we reach that land, we have to make our way down across the gully."

I cracked my eyes open and peered over the edge. Craggy rocks covered in thick green moss cut through the otherwise inviting valley.

"I can take a hint," I said, picking up my stick and hoisting myself up.

"Was that a hint?" he said, unsure, making me laugh again.

"We better get on with it if we hope to cross before nightfall."

The crossing took a lot longer than we thought with my injuries. The sun was high, signaling midday before I made it to the other side.

Sweat dripped from my brow from the effort of climbing. Shroding was patient, though, helpful and kind as he always was. Still, I could tell Shroding was getting anxious. We had been walking for well over a day.

His anxiousness did nothing for my own tipping emotions. I was in physical pain. I was heartbroken in more ways than I could count. The fragments of my mangled heart and mind only found solace in his kindness and patience towards me. A kindness and patience I attributed to my usefulness to him. I had one purpose, to bring him back. For the moment that was enough. It was enough for me to reject Shroding's offer to make camp after the arduous journey across the gully. It was enough to keep my feet moving even as my legs strained under my weight and my shoulder throbbed with the effort I expended pulling myself across to the other side. My one purpose was enough to keep my feet moving the whole rest of the day.

When we finally did stop, it was under a dense wood that

dimmed the light of the day even without a leafy canopy. Shroding had implored me to rest for a while, eat and build up my strength for the final stretch to Palace Moreh, believing it to be only another two days despite our slow pace.

I sat against a fallen tree.

"I'm going to go back to the gully and fill the canteen with water. I won't be gone long, will you be okay?" Shroding asked, looking at me for a long moment, his eyes holding the same concern they had carried all day.

"Please stay with the camp," he said lightly. "You are still injured," he continued. "You need to rest that leg. No needless moving around, got it?"

"Yes, my king." I bowed my head, jokingly.

"Hmm, I like that." He laughed. "Please refer to me as your king from now on."

I wanted to glare at him but found the whole exchange ridiculous. "Ha!" I threw a twig at him and then sobered. "Wait, seriously?" I panicked. He was the king. Technically I should be speaking to him far more formally, but the memories of him as my friendly neighborhood cat Iri, my chicken-poaching shadow, seemed to always outweigh how I should treat him. And yet, there was no denying who he was anymore. I wondered again how many more ways our relationship would change when he became human.

"No, I would not make *you* call me that," he said lightly. "But throw a twig at me again, and I'll have you beheaded." He laughed in earnest, and I could not help my feeble heart, which danced at the sound.

"You need me," I retorted with a smile.

His voice softened. "That I do." Something in the timbre of his voice made me wonder if there was more to it. And just like that, my heart puttered to life, and I felt the question that lay deep in my heart surface once more, a question that only a word from him could satisfy. "I'll be back soon. Stay out of trouble," Shroding warned, humor still in his tone, as he disappeared into the trees.

I closed my eyes, the struggle across the gully catching up to me as I drifted off to sleep.

———

Pocket Dimension

I woke up under the tree in the spirit dimension.

"Shroding?" I called, and within seconds he was there.

"You fell asleep fast," he pointed out.

"That gully was quite a workout," I teased, massaging my arms. At least in this dimension I did not have the aches and pains from all the attacks.

"Aren't you glad you stayed back at camp?"

"I suppose."

"Listening to your future king pays off from time to time," he offered taciturnly.

I shrugged. "I suppose."

He dropped down next to me, leaning back against the tree his face turned towards mine. Our shoulders pressed my body warming at the contact.

"Hi," I breathed self-consciously, fingers itching to fiddle with my hair.

He had been very attentive since the wolf attack, and the way he was always watching me gave me a nervous excitement.

"Hello?" he said calmly.

"So is it my turn to ask questions?" I hedged.

"What questions do you have?"

"More than I can say, but let's start with the court? What else should I know about these old guys, other than they live a really long time? How do they join the court?"

"Well, for one, don't call them old guys." He smiled. "To be a part of the king's court, you must be asked by the king. If you accept, then there is a ceremony."

"What happens at the ceremony?"

"It's a secret." He winked. "Part of what makes the court so different is that we are bound by our words. We take oaths to prove loyalty to the king. That oath is binding. Once the oath is made to serve the king, you are a part of the king's court until you renounce it or the king takes it away. Long life and increased power are the perks. Still, it's not without its costs."

"Costs?"

"Well, yes, once in the court, if you make a vow or oath to anyone, not just the king, you are bound to it. Should you break an oath, you are forced out of the court. You lose the long life and your gift entirely."

"Oh, so an oath is like life or death. That could easily be used against you. I mean, someone could force you to make an oath for something bad."

"Yes, it is a weakness, but it is also a true test of loyalty. People are selfish by nature; to give an oath is to give someone power over you, it is to give up control, to give up yourself. It's a beautiful thing, and an honorable one."

I could understand the beauty in it, but it still seemed dangerous. Giving an oath and breaking it would be like losing your family and your career all on the same day. I knew what that felt like. Flashes of the farm burning slipped into my *mind. The letter the soldiers had given me. An oath was not something to give lightly.*

"How do you end an oath?"

"Three ways: fulfill it, break it, or be released from it."

"Who can release it?"

"The person you gave the oath to."

I nodded. "What happens when you fulfill it? I mean, how do you know?"

"You are getting so serious. You don't need to worry about it." He unwound my hands, which had clenched my long braid. He held them, looking me in the eyes. "Oaths and the court are not things you need to concern yourself over. That's my job as a king." His smile was reassuring, but I was uneasy. I wasn't a part of the court. I could not make an oath, so why was I so anxious? Was it because Shroding could make an oath? Because he could vow something and give someone so much power over him? What happened if the king broke an oath? Did he lose his right to be king?

"Have you ever given an oath?"

"No, never." He sighed and then winced.

"How is your cut?" I asked, alarmed, my hands fluttering over his chest, not sure if his cut would even be visible in this dimension.

He looked down at me, brushing my hands away. "It's okay, mostly just bruises. The cut wasn't very deep." He frowned, his eyes falling to my shoulder. Gingerly he reached out, but hesitated. "May I?"

"Sure," I said, scooting closer to his outstretched hand.

He examined the tender flesh of my collarbone with featherlight touches that made my heart race. I could feel the bruising, but none of the marks were visible in the spirit dimension. So that answered my question. His fingers inspected my shoulder as if the marks could be seen, and he traced the skin like it was the most breakable thing he had ever touched.

He came closer, our hips pressing together. I clenched my hands in my lap, willing them to stay put. I wanted to touch him too. I had shamelessly fantasized about touching him. Feeling the warmth of his skin, not in this spirit world but in the physical. In reality with him as a human. Running my fingers through his twisted dark brown locks. Touching the hollow behind his ears with my lips. I wondered if touching him in real life would feel as electric as it did in this dimension. Would the sound of his voice hold the same delightful ring that sang out to me in this world? When I could hear the texture of his voice, not in my head, but from his own lips. Would he be more clear in a world that was more tangible?

His hands dropped, skimming the loose linen fabric at my waist, making me hot and frazzled. How could he be so oblivious? Did he truly feel nothing when he touched me? I looked up to see his gaze was intense but sad.

"I'm sorry," he said sombrely, tone like that of someone resigned for punishment.

"What?" I asked, endlessly confused.

"I'm sorry about your family, I'm sorry about your home and I'm sorry that your involvement with me has caused you so much harm. I know that is why you kept me away before at the shed, even as you cried alone. Honestly I don't blame you; I understand and am grateful you kept me away. We should not get any closer. It doesn't benefit either of us. I have done more damage to you than anyone I have ever known my whole four hundred years." He pulled back, standing, and turned away from me. "Don't call me to you anymore unless the

Wraiths have shown up. I can't. I can't bear it if I hurt you again."

I stood, taking in his words, feeling my heart ache and break and spring to life all at the same time. "I care for you," I said simply. "I kept you away not because I was mad, but because I didn't want you to see how much I was hurting. I thought you would blame yourself. Everything that has happened has happened because it had to. You said that too, before. I understand it now. I do not regret you coming into my life. I do not regret any of this." I gestured loosely between us, though he was not looking.

"I do." He sighed, turning slowly to look at me over his shoulder. To my horror, the regret was there in his voice, in the way he ran his fingers through his dark hair. "Still, I don't think I can..." He trailed off, looking pained. My heart beat in my chest like a drumstick, my body the skin of the drum shaking with every beat, as if one beat too hard would rip the skin, ending the rhythm forever. "Keep... from caring about you. I had thought I could draw a line. I thought we wouldn't cross it. You have no idea how hard it is to be a cat around you in reality," he confessed, his voice low. "The line keeps getting so blurry. It's too easy, being with you." He turned fully to face me, his brow furrowed.

"So why have a line at all?" I pleaded.

"Haya." He paused, looking for the right words as the silence weighed heavily on me. "I like being your friend." It wasn't just a statement of fact, it was a question and an appeal. He was asking to stay my friend, for me to not push him for more.

The flutter in my heart stopped, and for a moment I thought it wouldn't start again. Embarrassment burned my cheeks. I tried to understand his rejection. Tried to see his perspective. Perhaps it was because he would become king? Perhaps I would never be good enough? How could I have been so naïve? I was not good enough for the king of Shamar. But friendship? Could I stop the turn of my heart that had begun to hope for more than just friendship? More than just this temporary agreement of helping him? I looked at the hope in his eyes. The hope that we could walk back over the imaginary line he had made. I couldn't deny him. He was my friend. I wanted that friendship too. I could not lose what he had become to me. The safety net he had replaced in my life.

"Of course." I smiled weakly. "Friends." I held out my hand as if to shake on it. As if shaking on it would do away with the emotions gripping my heart.

His returning smile was warm. "Friends." He took my hand and held it, a soft look in his eyes that made me doubt friendship was truly all he wanted. I shook the thought away, and the dimension splintered around me. As if the spirit dimension knew I wanted out. Knew I wanted to leave.

"See you on the other side."

He nodded, letting me go and stepping back.

CHAPTER 17

Making Flames

I leaned on the log, looking up at the leafless canopy. I had been awake for only a few moments. When I realized Shroding was not back yet, I limped around, gathering dry wood for a fire. I had practiced a lot with Shroding to make fire, and even though I still had to use him as a conduit each time, I was determined to do it myself.

After the kindling and logs were stacked, I focused on my breathing, focused on the present moment and not on the ache in my chest. I focused on the rise and fall of my breath. It took longer than I would have liked, but the hum and colors came back. I looked around the vibration dimension, my own power pricking at my fingertips. Slowly it moved up my arms and filled my whole body. Warm. So warm. Like the feeling I would get at the Celebration of Strings each year. A time for family and memories and laughter.

Since we had left Wycliff, time had been lost to me, days and nights a blur. How soon was the celebration? Maybe only a week or so away? Memories of celebrations past filled my mind's eye, and my focus began to splinter at the sound of my mom gently playing the violin, while Theo and I wrapped ourselves up in a blanket, sipping hot cocoa. My father, stoking the fire and kissing my mother's cheek.

I shook my head, clearing away the memories.

I concentrated, breathing deeply and reaching for the string inside me. The pinpricks of power wove through my hands, coming into my core. I was not sure how to start the fire, but I wanted to try and see if I could summon the flame as Shroding had. I pushed the power out of me as I had been practicing. Thinking back to what Callum had shown me with Krav, I used the bend and flow of my hands, weaving and pulling the vibrations into the air in a steady wave, merging the Krav movement and the meditations practice Shroding had guided me through. Then, unsure if it was right, I opened my eyes to see if the fire had appeared.

Nothing. The stack of leaves and twigs were utterly untouched. So I tried again. This time as I moved through the flow, guiding the ribbons of vibration through the air, I had them rub against each other, the vibrations mingling and crashing over each other, till the power grew too chaotic for me to control and it burst out in a pop that had me falling on my butt. I winced, catching myself on my good arm.

"What am I doing wrong?" I groaned aggravatedly. What did I need to do to create the flame?

"Haya, what are you doing?" Shroding called in my mind.

"Nothing." I pouted. "Just practicing."

"I'm coming back to camp."

I crossed my arms. I could do it. I just needed to concentrate. But on what?

I looked at the leaves, plucking one from the pile and twisting it between my fingers.

Everything has a vibration, a frequency it gives off. If I could tap into their vibration, I could affect it with my own. Everything gives off something; even dead things have energy to tap into.

Closing my eyes, I blocked out everything but the sound of my breath. I blocked out the throbbing in my leg and arm. I blocked out the wind in the trees. I focused on the air filling and leaving my chest. Behind my closed eyes the sunlight vanished, the reddish tint of the sunset behind my lids going black.

The nothingness was cold, quiet, like wading through ink on all sides.

Then a spark of light expanded from the dark. Strings rolled out all around me. It was all too bright, too blaring, the colors and sounds merging in a pattern and rhythm, like a song I knew deep inside but had never heard, colors I could never dream of or imagine. I sifted through, seeking the strings tied to the leaves. If the darkness had been like wading through ink, moving through the light was like floating on a crystal clear lake, effortless and relaxing. As if the strings understood my desire, they floated up to meet me.

As I had done before, I pulled the king's power through me, centering it towards the strings in front of me. With a clear exhale, I pushed the power out, letting it tie to the vibration of the leaves. They tightened and burst, the energy shifting.

A loud pop had me opening my eyes, the vibration dimension falling away like sand on the wind.

I shook slightly but not from the cold, because red and orange flames licked and consumed the leaves before me.

I squealed with excitement. I had done it!

A rustle of branches behind me had me turning, my

achievement written across my face in a wide grin. "Look, I made fire!"

Dark eyes bore down on me, but they were not Shroding's.

"That little display of power has told me everything I needed to know. You are the one, and I know someone who will be delighted to meet you."

"Miles?"

I tried to stand, but there was no time, as he was already upon me, fist in the collar of my shirt.

With his injuries, he shouldn't have been able to breathe, let alone follow us across the gully.

He coughed up blood, and I could tell he was indeed dying, but prolonging the process by pumping his power into himself, by becoming like the Grieving.

"He is coming for you. He already knows you're here. It's only a matter of time."

I drew the gift up and channeled the power into my arms. I knew enough Krav by now. At least enough to get free and maybe even take down this already dying man. Unfortunately I was injured too, adding to the points stacked against me.

I threw my first punch. I kept my fist relaxed, careful as Callum and Shroding had taught me not to lock my arms.

With a fumbling twist, I swiped at his legs, the heel of my good leg landing with a crack against his shin. He grunted, head thrown back, and stumbled as he let go of my collar.

I rolled clumsily away, righting myself with the help of a nearby tree. I needed to buy time for Shroding to get back. The gully wasn't so far away. Could I make it to him? Blood seeped through the bandage around my leg. My shoulder throbbed from the impact of my punch. I wouldn't be able to hold out long.

I took a steady breath.

"I don't know who you think is looking for me, but if they are anything like the crowd you run with, I think I'll pass on the introduction."

Miles laughed. His jaw hung at a weird angle, but he didn't even look to be in pain. It was strange; any normal person would be howling in agony.

He stood to his full height, the firelight illuminating the stretched and peeling look of his skin. I covered my mouth, swallowing bile. Vibration sickness took longer than a few hours to have this kind of effect. What did it mean that he was already decaying so quickly? He was not a Grieving yet, not mindless. I realized then how bright the fire was, and how dark the woods had become. Night had fallen.

"We are well past introductions," he said, his words so slurred I almost couldn't understand him.

Then his eyes turned violet, and in a blur he charged me.

The vibrations were so powerful that even without my trying I could see them rippling around him in waves, completely encasing him to the point the man was gone.

I couldn't win against a Wraith.

I screamed, it was the only thing I could do.

A brilliant white horse galloped between me and the Wraith. I couldn't dwell on that, though, as I ran as fast as I could manage, warm blood pooling between my toes. I had to get away, had to draw the Wraith away from Shroding, so instead of running to the gully, I ran the opposite direction. Whoever Miles had said was looking for me might not yet know about Shroding. I intended to keep it that way.

I did not know how long I ran, or how far. But even as I

stumbled forward tripping, screaming the whole way down, I was hoping it was far enough. Enough to keep Shroding safe.

Even as the defining crack of ice and water erupted around me, my thoughts were on him, calling on the Creator to keep Shroding alive, to protect him. To give him another way to become human again. As I sank deeper into the freezing water, disoriented and unable to move.

Ice covered my skin, and I was swallowed up in seconds.

Water filled my lungs.

CHAPTER 18
Hold Your Breath

Water wrenching from my lips, I was vaguely aware when my head broke the surface. The churn of liquid sloshed in my ears as the water parted around me. An iron ring was around my waist as my head rested on... a rock? I couldn't tell. Was I alive?

"Hey! Stay with me," an unfamiliar voice said gruffly. Suddenly the iron ring and rock were gone as I became aware I was lying down. I struggled to breathe, a horrible scratching persisting in my lungs and nose, making it impossible to take a breath. Something warm came close to my face. I convulsed. Water spilled down my cheek as I turned my face. I wheezed. My eyes flicked open to see the gold color that had moved towards me underwater. I hadn't imagined it.

"Oh! Thank the Strings! It's okay, just breathe. I've got you." The voice was not in my head. I started, alarmed that this stranger was talking to me; actually talking. The texture of his voice was rough, unlike the smooth tones of Shroding's voice.

"W-What?" I gasped, but I didn't think he heard me over my haggard breathing.

Who was he? His gray eyes were wide, blond brows knit in concern. Then reason slipped in as his face came into focus. I knew this voice, this face. A flash of Shroding's memories from so long ago slipped in behind my eyes. The commander who'd invaded my camp.

"Callum?" I attempted, but I wasn't sure the name came out.

My lips were numb, so I couldn't be sure they had moved at all.

Callum carefully watched the emotions flickering over my features—recognition, then confusion—his own face changing in kind, from concern to hard and impassive.

My mind still felt like it was swimming, and though my breathing was better, my body was heavy, like salty water was sloshing around in every crevice of my body. My eyes closed, and I listened to the whistle of my inhales and exhales until consciousness left me.

———

When I woke, I felt like a juiced lemon. Dry and shredded. Which was befuddling after being sticky and wet for so long.

I did not remember being so warm when I had drifted, but as I came to, I smelled fire, lemon balm and honey in the air.

"Haya." Shroding's gentle voice soothed me, and I turned on my side, groaning. "You still have a fever, go back to sleep." A small but firm pressure rested on my forehead, and I decided that if Shroding was with me, then it was all okay, so I drifted once more.

―――――

Pocket Dimension

I was in a valley, large mountains behind me and a sprawling lake before me. Each time I entered the spirit dimension, I always appeared wherever I was asleep. Regardless of whether I was in a structure or not, I was always outside. It was a bit disorienting but helpful too—I could at the very least understand that I was somewhere new.

I called for Shroding.

I smiled when I saw him. Relief filled me as I took in his tall, lean form. He was okay. He was safe from Miles.

However my relief faltered because he was looking at me with utter terror in his dark eyes. As if a horrible monster was hiding nearby me. I glanced around, confused. The dimension was glowing with light, no trace of Wraiths anywhere. I stood and began to walk over to him.

He was shaking.

"Shroding?"

I was within arm's reach of him, and when I lifted my hand to his face, he blinked, and the turmoil was gone. His eyes focused on mine.

His hand covered my fingers, and he sighed. With his free hand, he cupped my cheek as I had done to his. Except he stepped closer, leaning down into me. His lips a breath from mine.

Was he about to kiss me?

My stomach fluttered with anticipation, but my mind fluttered to understand what I had missed.

I tilted my chin, but instead of a kiss, he rested his forehead against mine, closing his eyes.

It was then I noticed the lines of water curving over his sharp cheekbones.

Shroding was crying?

I tried to pull back to get a better look at him, but he would not let me budge an inch. He tugged me into his arms, every centimeter of my body flush against his.

Unsure what was wrong, I hugged him back.

"Everything is okay," I whispered.

I searched my memory for what would have made him so upset. Miles had attacked me, and I ran, and I fell. Ice water and Callum. Callum had saved me. I had been drowning. Then I woke up? Shroding had said I had a fever. Had I gotten sick? Was he worried about me? Had that made him so upset?

"Yes." His voice was hoarse. "Yes." He shivered in my arms. "You died. I felt you die." He made a sound like biting back a sob.

Desperate to stop his pain, I pulled away. "I'm okay, see?" I held out my arms, and though his tears had stopped, his face was still anguished.

My heart jumped as he grabbed me roughly again, drawing me tightly into him. My whole body was swallowed by his, and I shivered, a wave of safety flooding my system.

I sighed into his chest, relishing the closeness.

"Don't do that again. Don't disappear like that. Don't go to a place I can't follow." He growled low, his voice holding the faintest quiver of uncertainty. He squeezed me harder. "It just had to be water." His voice dripped with sarcasm. "I couldn't even get to you, to help you, all because of my... density issue," he grumbled bitterly. "It was maddening."

I listened to his confession in silence. A mix of guilt at making him worry coupled with delight that he had worried so much for me. He cared about me, but did he only care because

I was the key to his humanity? His request to just be friends tapped at my heart, interrupting its racing rhythm, with a warning. "You are just his friend, a tool, a means to an end," it whispered.

I tensed in his arms. He would be in big trouble if I had drowned. I tried to ignore the thought, but it made sense.

Shroding pulled back slightly, sensing my change. "What is it?" he asked, and I could feel his deep eyes searching my face, willing me to look up at him. When I didn't, he stepped out of our embrace and lifted my chin, forcing me to meet his gaze. "Haya?"

"It's nothing," I said flatly. "I'm just sorry I worried you. I know you still need me, and, well, I'm sorry." I shrugged. Everything teetered on him becoming human again. So many lives depended on it. I could not be selfish; he was not mine to keep.

His jaw clenched and unclenched like he wanted to say something, but he settled on, "You're impossible," and then his lips were over mine. It was so sudden, so delicious, I was completely stunned.

Shroding was kissing me.

It was so soft, tentative, curious even as his shoulders trembled against my palms from holding himself back. It was nothing like the kiss I had pinned him with so long ago, impulsive and hard. No, this one was a slow steam, like a sunshower hitting stone on a hot summer day. It was refreshing, cooling, and testing in its intensity.

The tension increased as his lips moved against mine, tantalizingly slow. Like a thousand years were passing by us with every gentle pressure, every breath. I had wondered before if during our last kiss he had kissed me back; now I knew for sure he hadn't, because Shroding was really kissing me now.

Last time it had been all me, my desire, my curiosity. This time we were in it together. His curiosity, my desire. It was like biting into a ripe peach. Perfection.

He closed the little gap between us by pressing his hand into my lower back, the other curling into the hair at my nape. He sighed, arms tightening, clutching me harder to his chest, as if there was still space between us. As if our bodies, wrapped around one another, were not close enough. I melted into him, hopelessly lost.

I was nothing more than lips and a body floating endlessly in his current.

He tugged softly at my hair, making me gasp. His tongue taking the opening and deepening the kiss. Strings, this was endlessly better than our first kiss.

The sensation from the last time coursed through me again. The hum amplified under my skin, splitting within my body. Electricity bounced through me like sparks contained in a jar. Wild and dangerous if not contained. And though the kiss was hungry, his tongue and teeth finding and taking, I knew Shroding was holding back, somehow, containing the electricity. I faintly recognized how similar the electricity felt to when I used the gift. Pinpricks across my skin, in my core, complemented by the drum of my heartbeat.

Shroding broke the kiss, my lips going cold.

My face was flushed and lips swollen when we separated. My whole body was shaking with a strange excitement that had me wishing I could keep him in this dimension, our secret place, forever.

My breaths were short gasps as air cleared my dazzled mind. I peered up at him, waiting for him to speak first, but he said nothing. His face was turned away, a pensive look in his flint eyes that was startlingly opposite from the euphoria no doubt glowing in mine.

We held each other, breathing in time. His hands still rested at my back and neck.

"Haya," he said softly, not looking at me. "I should not have done that." I took in his words like the slow drip of a faucet. Each splash washing away the rose glow the world had taken on.

I... drip. Should... drip. Not... drip, cut through my ears, sliced down my chest, creating a deep gash that resonated with rejection and confusion. After the intensity of the kiss we'd just shared, this was the last thing I'd expected him to say.

"Oh." I exhaled, stepping back and out of his arms. "I see." I didn't. I didn't understand how anyone could respond to a kiss like that, the way he had. Emotions washed over me like the rush of water that had threatened to drown me earlier. Rejection, confusion, and embarrassment filled my lungs till breathing became hard. I wanted to get away from him, to get away from myself too. I wanted to curl up inside myself. I wanted to disappear.

"Haya, please..." He reached for me, his hands trembling. I tried to understand his next words, but it was like I was hearing them from underwater. "The world has gone mad. You died. And Miles and the marauders, slave traders so deep into the kingdom, and the Grieving coming to your farm from the front line thousands of miles away. None of that should be happening. Shamar has fallen to darkness." His desperately pained expression ripped my heart further. "It's like you thought moments ago: so many lives depend on me. I'm supposed to save Shamar. Save everyone." His brow furrowed as he pleaded with me. Pleaded for something I couldn't understand. "But when I'm here with you..." His voice broke.

"I forget all of that. I forget all of it. Don't you see? It's wrong. I am a king. I have more battles to come after this one. I can't lose focus, be overtaken by jealousy, lust, possession, love, friendship, Haya, I—" But before he could finish, I turned my back to him so he could not see my face as the tears fell uselessly. I knew he could feel my pain through our connection. The torture he must be experiencing over his kingdom falling to ruin was probably crushing, and mixing with my pain till he couldn't tell where mine ended and his began anymore. Till we were both being swallowed by it. I understood him.

"I will help you get free," I whispered thickly. "I will do whatever it takes to make sure you are free and human again as I promised." I glanced at him. "But..." I hesitated, thinking, negotiating. I needed to be sure this intensity was something I could live without. I needed to be sure the passion between us was really just in this dimension, because of the king's power tying us together. "I have a condition."

The sorrow in his gaze was replaced with surprise, then his eyes narrowed, and even though I could tell he misunderstood, clearly not hearing my last thoughts, I let him think what he wanted.

The passion and worry for me cooled, shifting and becoming businesslike, aloof. "I can compensate you, of course." His tone was as frigid as the water in the lake. "Though I can't bring your family back, I can make sure you want for nothing in this life. If you wish, I can add you to the king's court. Should you desire a long life? As your life was almost lost, it's the least I can do." His tone was a mix of bitterness and understanding. It baffled me; did he think I wanted riches, more power? I would never try to extort from him. "You are doing a great service to the Kingdom of Shamar and should be compensated for such. Tell me what you desire, and I will swear an oath to give it."

I tried to ignore the harsh look in his eyes, dropping my gaze to his boots. I fiddled the end of my long braid nervously. "A kiss."

He stepped back as if pushed. "What?" His face twisted, completely appalled. I would have laughed but was too embarrassed to do anything but fidget with my braid.

"When you are human again," I finished, sucking in my lower lip, tasting his kiss with my tongue, desperate for more. Knowing more might very well break me.

He was as still as a statue, his eyes fixed on my mouth. My skin sizzled.

"Why would you want something like that?" His voice sounded hollow and distant.

"I..." I couldn't tell him it was because I wanted to know if it felt as electric in the physical world as it did here. I couldn't tell him it was because I was falling in love with him. I couldn't tell him it was because he was becoming family to me. Someone I could rely on, someone I could trust and someone I could give my whole life in devotion to because these feelings were too strong. These feelings were more about me than about him, because these feelings were still young to my heart, and I did not trust them. Because I hoped that by the time I turned him back into a human I would have these things sorted out. Because I would know at that point if I could love him and if he could love me too. "It's what I want," I said softly, recalling his promise to ensure my next kiss was one I wanted. I didn't want there to be any question about that, this time or the next. I wanted him. "It's the only thing I will ask you for, please... don't ask me why."

He leaned down to be level with me, his face a mix of

disappointment, comprehension and something else. He did not break his gaze even as his eyes flashed.

Casually he leaned in, his face a breath away from mine again, and I wished I were braver. Stronger, as to not let hope creep into my heart at his nearness.

"You are only hurting yourself by making such a request," he said. His tone was sullen, even as his eyes were sharp. Keen on seeing, knowing everything rolling around inside me.

I swallowed. "I know." The sound was nearly inaudible. I was a fool.

"I don't like to see you hurt, yet you ask me to?" His brow furrowed, but he backed up, giving me space. With deliberate slowness he put his fist over his chest. "I will give you what you asked for. Once I am a human again, I will kiss you. I give you my oath."

I nodded, my whole body flushing, grateful that the world seemed to fold in around me, sending me back to the dimension I belonged in. His oath a seal over my heart, only to be lifted by his lips.

CHAPTER 19
Coinania

"**M**y sister was out looking for the person who made a fire at the shed, our closest outpost..." The voice faded away.

I jerked upright, nearly falling off a small cot. I was no longer outside under a tree in the woods but in a large tent. Its curved white fabric danced with shadows from the oil lamps on the floor. Rugs of warm-colored patterns lined the ground, and a small table sat next to me with herbs and various bowls of liquids. The fabric of the tent rustled, and the person whose voice I'd heard walked in.

"Oh, you're awake," she said, her voice surprised.

The first thing I noticed was her long dark hair, then the tight linen bandages around her arms and face. She wore thick pants and boots dipped white with snow. The black fur of her vest contrasted the bindings around her face.

"We were a bit worried, your fever was quite high." I took in her words slowly, recalling the escape through the woods and my separation from Shroding. "You are very strong, so I knew you would come around." I could hear the smug smile in her tone but couldn't see it.

"A cat, was there a cat with me?" I asked, panicked, eyes searching the tent for Shroding.

She tilted her head. "Well, yes, actually. We brought the cat in, he was quite injured. I'm glad to know he is yours; we had you together in the infirmary, and when he saw you, he immediately climbed over to your bed and stayed with you. Everyone thought it was weird." She laughed. "Makes sense now that I know he's your pet."

Shroding was here, he was safe. But who were these people? Where was I? Why did he trust these people when he said we needed to stay away from everyone? "Where am I?"

"You're on the other side of Mount Arythma. Coinania to be exact."

"Coinania?" I asked, genuinely confused. I had never heard of such a place in all of Shamar, but then again, the only place I had even traveled to was Tyndale as a little girl. I shook my head slightly.

"Wow, you really don't know who we are. I didn't quite believe we were an unknown people. I was born here, you see. Never left once." She held up one finger for emphasis and came over to sit next to me on the cot. I pulled away unconsciously. "Hey, it's okay. We aren't gonna hurt you." She soothed, unfazed by my rudeness.

"I know the whole map of Shamar, and I have never heard of people in the mountains."

"My parents came from Golan—" She covered her already hidden mouth. "I shouldn't have said that." Her soft honey colored eyes flicked away. A color indicative of

Golanites. Was her skin wrapped to hide the notorious ashen pallor of the Golan people?

I pulled my knees to my chest. "Where is my cat?" I insisted, not sure what to make of her slip and her overly friendly disposition.

"Dunno. I haven't seen him. The elders were freaking out when they saw him, though. I've never seen a cat like him before. He looks more like a fox." She reached over, taking a bowl of liquid on the table, and held it out to me. "I'm Lev." She tapped my knee with the bowl. "This is medicine." I could hear her smile through the wrappings.

I took the bowl. "I'm Haya."

"Cool, your name means 'life' to my people. I like it. Mine means 'heart.' Life and heart, yes, very cool. I've never had a friend like you before. How old are you?"

"Seventeen, you?" I blinked, taking a hesitant sip of the liquid.

"Fifteen. I just got the gift a few months ago. You must be really talented, having had it for two years already. I'm still struggling to learn Krav."

"Well, I'm not that great," I hedged.

She tilted her head, unconvinced. "No way, your gift is so powerful, everyone felt it when you arrived. My sister was saying you're stronger than Mama Meod. She came from Golan—er, sorry."

"Why do you do that?"

"Dad always told me that people outside don't like Golanites."

"I've never met a Golanite before," I answered honestly. Who was I to judge a people? "Shamar has been fighting Golan for a long time," I added. I couldn't judge a people, but I also couldn't deny the facts.

"We aren't like the things Shamar fights. We are escapees, you see." She leaned in closer and whispered, "We were slaves."

"Slaves?" My brow furrowed. King Roark had abolished slavery of every kind and had very strict laws preventing anyone from owning another person. "I don't understand?"

She reached for the knot under her vest and pulled up, unraveling the bandages on her face. Her skin was very pale, the undertone like light-colored soot in a fireplace. She was young, with round cheeks and a small mouth. She smiled, showing off two very deep dimples.

"I know we look kinda funny to you. But I'm sure you can see we aren't like those with vibration sickness." She touched her face self-consciously.

It was my turn to tilt my head. She was right. She looked nothing like those with the sickness. Nothing like the decaying things that had burned down my home. She was different, no doubt about it, but not violent, not roiling with hate and murderous intent. She was just a girl. Like me.

"You don't look funny. You're cute. Really pretty." I returned her smile. "Thank you for helping me recover."

Her dimples deepened. "You're way prettier than me." She shuffled her feet, embarrassed. "I've always wanted to make a friend from the outside."

"Well, you have one," I affirmed, my mind drifting back to my other friend. Shroding, the one I had coerced into making an oath to kiss me. If I had been alone, I would have slapped myself for being so foolish. He was probably mad at me. "I really do need to find my cat." My voice was edged with panic again.

"I'm right here." Shroding's voice filled my mind, and I turned my head to the side as his face pushed through the flap in the fabric. His dark eyes drank me in. He looked so healthy, the stitches gone as if he had been healed.

"Oh, look," Lev said, jumping up. "Hi, kitty." She reached out to pick him up, but he dodged her, jumping on the bed next to me.

"He's fast."

"Yeah, he's not a fan of being held," I offered, petting him to keep up appearances of him being my "pet."

He rolled his head from under my hand to avoid my touch and faced Lev.

"At least not as a cat," he teased, flicking his tail in my face. I blinked, surprised. Was he flirting? Inconceivable! For a moment I was not sure who he was flirting with. It wasn't like Lev could hear his teasing.

"May I pet him?" Lev asked, eyeing Shroding with wonder.

"Oh, um..." I hesitated, unsure how Shroding felt about being treated like an actual cat. She held out her hand as Shroding lifted his head, rubbing against her fingertips. And here I thought petting him was *my* thing.

"Aw, he is so cute!" She knelt, going all in on petting and scratching. I tried to hide my laughter as she bombarded him with affection.

Shroding glanced at me. "What is so funny? She is a cute kid and doesn't know any better."

I flinched at his assessment. She was only two years younger than me. If she was a kid in his eyes, then did he also see me that way? Was I just a kid to him? I pulled my hair around my neck, plucking absently at the ends.

"So, Lev, not to be rude, I'm grateful for your help, but I'm headed to Tyndale and should probably be on my way soon."

"Wow, I've only ever seen Tyndale's city lights." She beamed, eyes wide. "But... you're still not one hundred percent. I don't think the village elders would be okay with you leaving in your condition."

"Haya, it's okay to stay here a little longer, they can take care of you," Shroding said calmly.

"Could you ask the elders for me, Lev?" I needed to talk to Shroding alone.

"Okay, I'll be right back. Don't go vanishing or something." She smiled, pointing at both me and Shroding before dipping out of the tent.

"Shroding, I thought we weren't supposed to be around people?" I whispered once she was gone.

"These people are different."

"Is it really okay to stay here, though?" I asked, still picking at the ends of my hair. "Won't the Wraiths catch up to us? This is a town... What if they are here, like you said?"

"Though the possibility of a Wraith attack is higher here than on our own, the Wraiths are afraid of the village chief, Mama Meod, so they wouldn't linger here. For now we are safe."

"How do you know they are afraid of her? Who is she exactly?"

"Let's just say this isn't my first time visiting this town." He nudged my hands, which were still picking at my hair. I stopped and looked at him. "You are safe. Just rest and heal a little," he said, a mix of concern and assurance in his voice. "You died, after all," he added dryly.

"Okay," I agreed, lying back down. "Shroding?"

"Hmm?"

"Stay next to me, okay?"

"I'll be here." He curled into my side. "In every dimension I'll be next to you," he promised.

I rested my hand over his back, feeling the thrum of his purr, and closed my eyes. My mind quickly became fuzzy and jumbled with sleep as the effects of the medicine set in. A faint whisper tapped in the back of my mind, words I couldn't quite hold on to.

"Even if you can't see me..."

———

This time I dreamed with a clarity different from the other dimension, as if I traveled back in time to when I was just a child, having left Wycliff for the first time at a mere seven years old.

I looked up at the buildings made of stone and wood, buildings much like in Wycliff, but these were taller, stronger, built to withstand the storms off the coast. Everything was so much bigger in the port city of Tyndale than in Wycliff. It was noisy, crowded, and I could smell the salt of the sea on the wind.

I watched the people move like cattle in and out of shops and alleys. The wind blew, twisting my blue dress, which was two sizes too big for my slight frame. I frowned, looking over to where my father stood with a merchant.

The merchant looked inconsequential in comparison to my father, who was the retired captain of the seventh rank, a revered war hero. A war that showed on his face with every wrinkle and scar. He was diligent in keeping himself clean-shaven; he said it was a habit from being in the military. Despite that, he kept his hair long, braided down his back, a streak of salt and pepper twisted through the dark plait. I listened to the murmurs of passersby as they looked upon my father. Though Tyndale, like Wycliff, was far from the battles, both cities had heard of my father. Heard of his heroic acts some thirty years ago before his injury. He had a limp, which he never discussed. He would tell story after story of war times but never that one. The limp did not diminish his impressive presence. His towering height and broad chest gave him an air of authority people unconsciously reacted to.

I frowned, not because people were staring and whispering about my father, that was not new; it was because he had promised to help me find a gift for Mom's birthday, but so far all we had done in the big city was talk to burly men with long white beards. I tried not to pout as my little legs carried me a few paces away. Still, I was careful not to lose sight of my father. I peered down an alley and saw a flower cart. The cart held so many colors, colors I didn't even know flowers could come in.

My mood instantly brightened at the thought of getting my mother flowers. The only flowers we had by our house were dandelions, but father always said they were weeds and did his best to pluck them from the yard regularly.

I walked to the mouth of the alley, drawn to the vibrant colors, forgetting that father had told me to stay close to him. A few paces in, I reached the cart and stood on my toes to inspect the flowers. I sniffed each one, trying to decide which one had the best fragrance. They were all like nothing I had ever smelled before in my seven years. I twisted the end of my hip-length braid, the gold locks coming loose around my face. I brushed them away, frustrated. I didn't know what flower mom would like best.

A woman yelped behind me, and I turned to see a lady in

a long azure gown pushing a large cat away from her with her boot. "What manner of beast are you? Shoo!" she cried.

The cat seemed large to my small body; the cats on the farm were small enough for me to pick up, but this animal could have easily carried me on its back. Perhaps it was a dog, its size much like the great hounds that stood guard at the Citadel. I decided it must be an odd species of dog by its peculiar pattern of black-and-gray fur and puffed tail. The poor thing looked hungry and scared. I didn't understand why the lady was being so cruel.

Forgetting the flowers, I moved over to touch the dog.

"I'm sorry, miss," I said, smiling brightly at her. "My dog just got away from me." I reached over to pet behind its triangular ears, but it cowered to the ground, looking past me. I followed its terrified gaze.

"Well, keep your creature on a leash next time." She fluffed her dress and moved to leave the alley.

At the opposite mouth of the alley stood a tall teenage boy. Just looking at him made me want to cry. He was lanky, with hard yellow eyes. I backed up instinctively. I glanced back at the dog, but it was gone. The young man strode towards me, his strides bigger than the length of my body. I backed up till I was against the flower cart; it rocked slightly behind me as I bumped it. Just as he passed, I whipped around, hiding my face in my hands against the cart.

I jerked back, stumbling over my feet as the hair at my scalp ripped slightly.

"Ah!" I cried, gripping my head.

The boy turned around, looking down at me and then at where my braid had caught on the buckles of his knee-high boots. Tears filled my eyes as he bent, one of his hands engulfing my upper arm and the other grabbing my hair. His nails bit into the skin on my arm as he held me in place to rip my unruly locks free from the buckles. My braid bunched at weird angles as a tuft of my hair broke off.

"Unbelievable," he hissed, eyes flashing from pale green back to yellow. He could have been handsome, but his face was too sallow and thin to be healthy.

"I-I'm sorry," I whimpered, my scalp aching and arm tingling with pain.

He glared down at me, unamused, still holding my hair in his hand. "Shall I save you some trouble in the future and cut this rat tail off for you?" He leaned closer, tugging my hair free of the plait, and smiled—at least I thought it was a smile. His teeth didn't look real, like they were made of paper.

"N-No, please, sir." My voice trembled. The clatter of glass rolling on the cobbled ground caught his attention, and he stood, forgetting me, and moved towards the sound.

I ran out of the alley as fast as I could, right into my father's legs.

"Haya, where were you! What were you doing, running off?" He scooped me up and held me to his broad chest. I sniffed, but did not cry. I curled up against his shoulder.

"Can we go home?" I whispered.

"Okay, okay," he soothed, smoothing my wild hair, saying nothing of the broken strands.

He turned and carried me away. I looked up from his shoulder at the dark alley, and though the yellow-eyed boy was gone, my skin prickled as though someone was still watching me.

<hr>

I gasped awake, wheezing through the full-body spasms that gripped me.

Shroding was at my side. "It's okay, Haya, it wasn't real, it was only a dream," Shroding assured me, head lifting from my side where he lay on the cot next to me in the tent. I was in Coinania. Right.

"I can't feel my arm." I panicked. "I can't feel it." Though, I was lifting it and moving it all around in a panic.

"It's okay. It just fell asleep, breathe. You are safe."

I took a few deep inhales, and the sensation returned to my arm. I was okay. I closed my eyes, lying back down.

"Right, right..." I sighed, letting the words soothe my pounding heart, and slept.

It had just been a nightmare.

No, my subconscious warned. It was real. Somehow I was sure it was very, very real.

CHAPTER 20
Mama Meod

"The leaders will see you now." Lev's voice roused me. "Oh! No, you're sleeping... I didn't mean to wake you." She covered her mouth as if she could undo waking me by muffling her voice.

"It's fine, I'm up." I sat, groggy, and rubbed my eyes. I pat the bed next to me but Shroding wasn't there.

"Your kitty is already down at the meeting." Lev came over, lifting a lantern to my face, making me flinch. "How's that fever? Are you feeling up to going outside?"

I nodded, turning to stand.

"Okay, here are some boots. The snow is rather deep tonight." She placed a pair of thick fur boots at my feet. "Oh," Lev said, jumping up and running over to a piece of fabric hanging by the fire. "I believe this is yours."

I took the green coat from her. It was the contraband Shroding had stolen for me and then Callum had accidentally taken.

What had happened to Callum?

Voices spoke outside the tent flap.

"Was she committing suicide?" a woman asked.

"I don't think so... She knew who I was. She could be a spy for..." The voice faded, and I recognized it as Callum's. I needed to address the confusion.

It was a good thing Shroding was not around.

Lev opened another flap on the opposite side of the tent. "I just need to grab a few things, then I can walk you over. Be right back," she said cheerfully, and disappeared down a long wooden corridor.

I stood, tucking my feet into the boots and slipping my arms into the fur coat.

Curious, I lifted the flap Lev had disappeared through. It had not been my imagination. There was a corridor. I walked carefully down it. The boards creaked under my boots, the space dark save for a lantern on either end of the narrow space. Where did it lead?

When I got to the end, it split off. A tent flap like the one I had left through was to my right, and another long corridor was to my left. I continued down it, getting lost at each turn. From what I could gather, it was a maze of tents, all connected by a string of passageways.

I was hopelessly lost and about to turn around when abruptly I was shoved back.

My feet slipped, as my boots were big and awkward on my feet. My head bounced against the wood wall, narrowly missing the iron wall lantern. I winced as the lantern swayed on the wood next to me.

Gold locks came into view. Callum's large hand grabbed my shoulder, straightening me and pinning me back, his knee pressing into my thigh. I gasped with pain as something sharp and cold lay against my neck.

"Who are you?" Callum hissed, holding a dagger at my

throat. I turned my face away. A second man came up from behind Callum, and though I should have been more concerned by the blade at my throat, I stared at the figure in the fleeting light, his face new to me. "Don't make me ask again." Callum shook me, bringing my attention back to him.

I knew more about Callum than about Shroding's other friends. From that knowledge I knew Callum wasn't bad—at least he hadn't been when Shroding knew him, but that had been two hundred years ago. Things could have changed as Shroding feared. Yet Callum had saved me twice. Those were good marks in my book. Though his holding a knife to my throat definitely didn't bode well.

I sent Callum a pleading look. Callum may have been Shroding's friend once, but it was obvious I was not his, and I guessed saving my life earlier didn't make us allies either.

"Commander," I whispered, trying to pull away from the hard metal.

"Oh, is it Commander now?" He glared, eyes full of distrust. "How do you know my name? I never gave it to you."

So he remembered my calling him Callum, then. I had no idea how I would explain that one. Instead I evaded.

"Thank you for saving me earlier," I said, rushing the words, not feeling their meaning.

The blade lifted, curving against my jaw. "Don't make me regret it. Now tell me who you are."

"Haya," I choked against the dryness in my throat. "My name is Haya Golden." I began to push slightly at his chest, trying to create distance from the knife. My throat still burned, and my mouth was gritty as if filled with sand. I sifted through my mind, trying to figure out what to say next.

The blade faltered slightly, the pressure lifting. "Where were you running off to? Disappearing like you did at camp?"

He shoved his free hand under my coat, searching me. "Stealing anything?" His husky voice was cutting, and I could feel the vibrations of it against my palms as I attempted to create distance between us.

"I got lost," I whispered.

"Clearly, you did not make it to Oro."

I lifted my gaze to his. His gray eyes were impossible to read in the faint lantern light. The pale eyes of the man in my dream and the pale eyes of the man who'd attacked Shroding... Were they the same person? Was Callum working with Skithian? I wished I could be certain.

"Callum!" Lev's normally sweet voice was booming with rage. "Get your hands off her this instant!"

"Stay out of this, Lev."

Lev appeared next to the boy behind Callum, and with one look, the boy scurried off. "I'm not going to ask you again."

"Lev," Callum warned, eyes sliding over to where she stood behind him.

She had her hands on her hips and a scowl that had me cowering a little.

Callum blew out a rattled breath and stepped back from me. In an instant Lev was in his face, poking his chest with an authority that had Callum wincing. Needless to say, I was thoroughly impressed.

"First you save her life, then you hold a knife to her neck. What kind of man are you? You should be ashamed. She is still recovering, and after all Mama Meod did for her." Her cheeks puffed up as she tilted her chin. "You would threaten her recovery for what? Huh? To question her? Why would you do that? Even if she were a spy or something, that is not how we treat people. You know better. If you want to behave like a pompous assassin, torturing and maiming people to get answers, then you can go back to your castle and do it there!" Her face was flushed by the end of her tirade, eyes blazing, and Callum, to his credit, looked rightly put in his place.

"Lev..." He said her name with a tenderness that even to my ears sounded rehearsed, as if he had to use that tone with her often. It sounded just like when Theo would try to butter me up or apologize for something. I covered my mouth to hide my laughter.

Callum didn't like that and glared at me. Still, he tucked his dagger away, and my shoulders relaxed.

"If you have questions for her, you will ask civilly after she meets with Mama Meod." Lev took my free hand. "Come on, Haya," she said breezily, pulling me past Callum.

She led me out through another tent and into the snow.

"Wow," I gasped, looking up at the wide open night. Snowcapped mountains glistened on all sides in the moonlight, and the lake looked like a sea in the darkness. The stars freckled the sky in glittering shapes I didn't recognize.

"The meeting hall isn't too far. I know it's pretty cold tonight, and you should be careful about getting too cold." She turned and winked at me.

I personally felt it was too soon to joke about my near drowning and hypothermia incident, but I knew she meant no real harm by it, so I said nothing.

When we reached the tent for the meeting, Lev smiled and told me she would meet me after it was over to take me back to her tent.

I didn't know what to expect, meeting Mama Meod, or what it would mean for our journey to Tyndale. But these people had saved me, and so I owed them a debt.

Steeling myself, I entered the shelter.

Inside, the tent glowed golden from a large and lively hearth in the center. On one side were living quarters, and before me was a sort of confluence of cushions each occupied by a fur-clad and skin-wrapped villager. All their faces were hidden despite their having to know I was already aware they were Golanites.

Only one woman—obviously Mama Meod by her seat, which was just slightly higher than everyone else's—left her face uncovered. She was marked by deep age lines, though her skin was unpitted or spotted. Her eyes were a rich honey, and like everyone else she wore a pattern of furs across her body. Her hands were also left exposed, showing the ashen undertone of the southern people.

"Haya?" Shroding's voice pulled my attention. He sat beside a vacant cushion for me. I came in silently and sat beside him as everyone watched, clearly waiting for something.

I chewed my lip. Shroding sensed my nerves and pressed his paws against my leg, rolling onto his side like he had done before on the cliff edge. The gesture was still so cute, and though I didn't laugh like last time, an unsuppressable smile lifted my cheeks.

"You love him very much." Mama Meod spoke, her voice charging the room with some kind of energy. I looked up, surprised. My face heated from her poignant observation. Was it that obvious?

Shroding glanced at Mama Meod, then at me.

I didn't want to address her too accurate comment, so I did the safest thing I could think of.

"Thank you so much for taking me in and nursing me to health," I said, bowing my head in respect.

"Child, I know who you are. I would only use my gift on someone so worthy."

I blinked. What gift did she mean, and what did she know about me?

"I'm sorry," I said, shaking my head. "If I may, how do you know me, and what do you mean by your gift?" I asked as politely as I could manage, curiosity making me excited.

"You have a great power, one that can turn the tide of this war, but only if you embrace it, not for the love of a man, but for the love of mankind."

I glanced at Shroding, unsure as to how she could possibly know he was actually a man, not a cat. Shroding did not look at me but stared at the older woman.

"A man from the king's court came here looking for your cat. Now why would someone of the king's court seek you out, child?"

I tilted my head, utterly lost. A man from the king's court? Who could that possibly be? Was *he* the man she'd mentioned before, not Shroding? Impossible, I didn't know anyone in the court.

"Mama, she seems rather confused," a man beside me offered.

Mama Meod leaned forward and smiled. "Very well. I healed you, child. That is my gift of vibration, one coveted by many and so rare that they would kill to have it. But this gift, like so many, is not without drawbacks. In healing you, I become part of you for the length of time the healing takes. I am able to see into you. Your most critical memories. I have seen your loss, and I have seen the beginning of your journey."

I gasped, fearing not only for Shroding's secret but also for myself. A strange feeling of violation washed over me, and my stomach turned to knots. This woman, without my knowledge, had done something I didn't even know was possible with the gift and, in doing so, had stolen something. A something I didn't have a name for, but I felt at the very core of me. My face scrunched in disgust. A twist of vulnerability and nakedness gripped me. I was laid bare, exposed before this woman, and though being known or truly seen should not have been a bad thing, it did when that knowing was not given by choice.

"You are mad? Though I saved your life?"

I soured at her words, ashamed. Wasn't I supposed to be grateful? Had I not just thanked them for saving me? Did that make it okay for her to take from me even as she gave?

I exhaled sharply. "I don't know what to make of all you are saying. I don't know who the man from the king's court is, nor what you saw, but I will say this." Shroding looked at me then, his eyes flickering iridescent. "I am on the side of Shamar, and as long as you do not stop me from seeing this kingdom restored, or from continuing my journey to Tyndale, we are on the same side, and though I don't feel comfortable with what you did, I have no desire to be angry with you."

Mama Meod laughed then, loud and booming, her small frail frame shaking with delight. "That is the spirit that can turn a kingdom and a heart." She closed her eyes and nodded. "The man you seek, even as he seeks you, is Callum McClain."

My eyes narrowed.

Her wrinkles lifted in a drooping pattern about her cheeks as she said excitedly, "Yes, the very one who saved you. He does not know what he is looking for just yet."

I glowered at her. Why was she speaking in riddles?

"As for your journey, we will set you up with provisions, but I encourage you, take some rest here for a day or two."

I opened and closed my mouth, unsure what to say. But Shroding answered for me, standing up and walking out of the tent, putting an end to the conversation altogether. I stood up too, nodded at the group and hurried to follow him into the night.

CHAPTER 21
Ten Years

Lev was walking up to the tent as I came out.

"Finished already?" she asked.

"Did you see my cat?" I said, looking around.

"No, you sure do lose him a lot." She laughed, and I bristled, knowing she didn't mean anything by it, but it wasn't an observation I enjoyed having pointed out.

"He's probably back at the tent," I said passively, and began walking in the direction I thought the tent was. Apparently I was correct because Lev got the point and hurried ahead to lead me the rest of the way.

"How did it go?" Lev asked, her chipper attitude making me twitch.

"I don't really want to talk about it," I grumbled, sure she must have known what Mama Meod had done.

"You know Mama Meod doesn't like to use her gift. She only does it when it's dire and she has no other choice."

I frowned deeper, unsure how Lev was able to pinpoint the very thing I did not want to talk about every time she opened her mouth. Maybe this was another special power of the gift? Something else I didn't know.

"I really would rather forget about it." I closed my eyes, trying to keep in mind that my life had been saved by these people.

"I can't understand fully, but I can imagine it is uncomfortable." She seemed to catch on to my displeasure. "Still, I'm glad you are alive." She smiled, her dimples darkening the corners of her mouth. "Don't let Callum get to you either, he really is a big softy most of the time."

"You seem pretty close," I mused.

She shrugged. "I've known him my whole life."

"Is that why you were able to tame his temper before?"

She laughed, light and playful. "By the Strings, no! If anything, because we are close he cares less what I say."

"How did you do that, then? It was pretty impressive."

She beamed at my compliment.

"I'm to be the next chieftain. My sister married the head of another family and as such abdicated her role. So..." She lifted her boot, crunching the snow heavily under her foot. "I'm next. Coinania is a sovereign state. Though we are part of the kingdom, we have our own laws and ways of doing things. The steward put it in place a few hundred years ago or so, Callum has to respect that." She crinkled her nose in delight. "I outrank him."

She outranked me—did that mean she was on par with Shroding? I supposed in a way she was like a princess to her people. The thought unsettled me. Especially with the way Shroding had behaved towards her. He would have to choose his future partner from people of her caliber, not a farm girl from the north, like me.

"I'm really tired," I said weakly, eager to talk to Shroding, and dreading it all the same. I hoped he was inside waiting for me.

Lev nodded, opening the tent flap. "I'll be sleeping in the tent next door." She pointed down the connecting structure that mazed between all the homes. The tip of the tent she referred to was visible and only a short walk away. "If you need anything," she offered, and wished me good night as I dipped inside.

Shroding sat on the bed, waiting for me.

"As Lev said, you aren't fully recovered yet, even if Mama Meod used the healing gift on you. The discomfort and soreness will still be there." He explained.

I nodded, the ache in my joints was apparent with every movement, and even though it had been an excuse to Lev, I was, actually, very tired. "What are we going to do?" I asked as soon as Lev had left. Sitting down next to him on the bed, I noticed his stitches were gone. "What happened? You're healed?" Without thinking, I roamed my hands over his body, investigating his chest and belly. He was unharmed.

After a beat he stepped back, sliding out of my reach. "I was healed as well."

Understanding dawned on me. "Do you think Mama Meod knows about you? From my memories, or yours?"

"She can only see the ones that have critically impacted your life." He spoke softly, and I hopped off the mattress, worrying my lip.

So then she definitely knew about him. Shroding had changed everything about my life. But what memory had she seen? Him as a prince? As a cat under the moonlight?

Shroding sat on the bed, watching, as I paced near the entrance. "They know about me, that I was born. They believe I'm coming back. As far as knowing that I am a cat and such, I can't know for sure, unless Mama Meod tells us what she saw, but it's best to assume she knows. However, they are on our side. We can trust her."

"How do you know that?"

"They want Skithian gone as much as we do. They have been on the receiving end of his cruelty and hunger for power. They understand better than anyone the pain he inflicts. The prince is their savior, their hope."

I made my way to the bed. "Then do you think Callum knows? He cornered me before the meeting. I guess I used his name, and now he is even more suspicious of me. Thinks I might be a spy." I laughed without humor. What was I going to do about his suspicions? Mama Meod had said he was looking for me and that he didn't know what he sought. Did that mean he was not aware of Shroding or that I had the king's power? Did that mean he hadn't been the one to betray Shroding before, the one who hurt him?

"Do I think Callum knows the prince is a cat? No. That the prince is still alive, yes, even if he is not the one who betrayed me. If he has spent any time with these people, then he would know their beliefs and be looking for me."

"Why can't we confront him? Couldn't he help us?" I wrung my hands as I sat down on the edge of the bed. "There has to be a way to know if he is really trustworthy. I had this nightmare while I was feverish, but it seemed more like a memory." Flashes of the dream filled my mind, making me more sure it was not a dream at all. I had gone to Tyndale when I was seven. I had never gone back. In fact, for years after, I had an irrational fear of the city. Perhaps it had not been so irrational after all. Was it a repressed memory?

"It's not that simple, I have my reasons for avoiding those I once knew." He shifted on the bed.

"Yes, the betrayal. You never told me... where it happened?" I placed my hand over his paw. "Was it in Tyndale"—I did simple math—"about ten years ago?"

His tail thrashed. "How would you know that?"

"A little girl in a blue dress," I muttered to myself. By the Strings, I had been there. I had seen his assailant, and that man was not Callum. "It wasn't him," I whispered, the memory becoming clear.

"Don't shut me out, show me what you are thinking," Shroding demanded, fangs bared slightly.

I focused, sending him some of the power as a way to deepen our connection. I let the memory flow through my mind. The way the young man had treated me. The violent look in his pale eyes. Callum and this man did look similar, but they were not the same. Callum was fuller, livelier looking, hair just the littlest bit darker.

The tent was quiet save for our breath, which was in sync as the images filled both our thoughts.

When it was done, Shroding growled, the sound full of regret and anguish.

"It was Logan."

"Logan?" I asked. "He tried to kill you?"

"That was my second encounter with him," he mumbled to himself, connecting dots in his mind I could not know. "He found out I was alive fifty years ago. At the time, I wandered freely from town to town, city to city, thinking I was safe. I didn't have the king's power, so I didn't draw any attention. I was just a cat, and it was fun..." His ears flattened. "I was outside the capital when he tracked me down the first time; it wasn't to capture me, though. When he found me, I was trusting, thinking I had found a friend, someone from my past who could help me. I had no way of communicating with him, so I led him to a clearing at night. He wanted proof that I was who he thought, so I walked into the moonlight, like a fool. He knew about my father's journals; the one in Wycliff was not the only one with that poem. Logan knew about the prophecy, he knew far more than he should."

"Fifty years ago?" I interrupted. "That was when forces from Golan burned the seven villages outside Romath. It was when the hundred and fifty years of peace ended and this new war began."

"Yes, the peace ended because Skithian found out I was still alive, which made his deal with my father void. I had always wondered if Logan was the one behind all of it, but I had no way to know for sure, until now."

"Then ten years ago?"

"I don't know how I was captured. I was drugged most of the time." He fumbled over his words, speaking slowly, almost disjointed as he pieced everything together. "All the memories are hazy, unclear. For over a week I was held prisoner, caged in a cellar. A low point for me, living off rats—when I was well enough to move, that is." He trembled. "I gathered that my captor was trying to figure out the process of the transformation. As I said before, I didn't know it was Logan, but your memory proves it. He has been the one after me. Looking for a way to give Skithian human form, for a way to complete the transformation of the Nephesh, as my father had done."

I shivered, recalling the ominous feeling Logan had given off in that alley years ago. "I don't understand—you're in another dimension, and Skithian's trapped because of your father's deal." Something drifted in my mind, like a piece of truth I had ignored. "... Right...?" I whispered.

"He is trapped in another dimension, like me. It is

reasonable to say he could be brought back through the same methods as myself."

"But you have a body." I gestured to his cat form. "Sort of."

"I would venture to say that as long as there was a host body for Skithian to inhabit..." He trailed off, not needing to explain more. My stomach rolled at the thought of someone giving up their body to a foul thing like Skithian. "Logan didn't know; at that time, I had no idea how I would be brought back."

"But now you do, right? At the palace?"

"Yes, Mama Meod has one of the king's journals, and inside is the list of conditions that must be in place for the transformation to occur."

"What?" I leaned forward. "What conditions?"

He shook his head, "We will have plenty of time to talk about those details." His dark eyes lifted to search mine, wonder and amazement filling them. "I told myself if I ever met that child again, I would thank her for what she did. I still can't quite believe it was you. In that dank alley. I was very grateful to the child who had protected me, but I had no idea who you would become." His ears flattened. "I didn't have the attention, then, to think about anything but survival." His dark eyes showed all the possibilities that were lost. He could have become human ten years ago. My family would still be alive. "I was so drugged. The world could have been on fire, and I would not have known. Yet even in my drugged haze I saw you. You were so small in your oversized blue dress, looking up at the flower cart. Your hair was long and braided, just like it is now." He tilted his head, looking at where my hands unconsciously held the plait.

I chuckled nervously, eyes wide. "It's weird being called a

child; I mean, we are the same—" I stopped from saying age, because that was not true. "We *look* the same age," I amended, blushing. "In your other form, I mean." I was digging myself into a hole.

He leaned up and pressed his cold nose against my cheek. His purr was loud and full. "Thank you, Haya, for what you did then and for helping me now."

I flushed from head to toe. "I-I didn't even know what I was doing then." I waved it off and in my embarrassment changed the subject. "So, um, what about Callum?"

Shroding pulled back assessing me for just a moment before accepting the redirect. "Yes, Callum..." Shroding hummed in thought.

"You didn't want to trust him because of the betrayal, right? Well, we know he was not that person, so can we tell him?"

"You already did," he muttered.

"W-What, when?" I stammered.

"While you were sleeping. You said my name. He knows you know where I am, or at the very least that you are connected to me. He will not let up until you tell him the full truth."

I exhaled. "Then I better go find him." I moved to stand, but Shroding hovered his paw over my shoulder.

"Tomorrow, Haya." He sounded tired, maybe even a little scared. "Let's sleep on this just one more night, please."

"Of course."

"Thank you."

I slipped off the coat and boots, setting them by the fire to dry. Silently I ran my fingers through my hair. The strap I had used to tie it back had fallen out at some point, but the knots in my hair had held the braid together. I glanced around the tent for anything I could use to tie off a new plait. I was snooping through Lev's stuff, when I found a brush and cord for my hair. I set to work. I'd thank her later. Slowly I rebraided the mess of strands. I had been braiding my hair since I was a child, and I fell into the deft movements even as my fingers strained with the intricacy. The simple act was grounding, making the events of the day feel far away.

Shroding silently turned down the bed for me, flicking the blankets back with his paw.

When I was finished I lay down next to Shroding, rolling over to face him. He ducked his head, resting it near mine.

"We are one step closer to bringing you back." I yawned.

He was quiet for a while. "I didn't believe in fate or destiny, but meeting you... well, I have wondered about a lot of things. Things that don't seem possible but are... with you."

"Is it odd that I feel the same way?" I asked, searching his eyes. My life had fallen apart since he came into it. I knew that, but still, even knowing that... knowing I should hate him for taking so many things away from me, for bringing me into a fight I wasn't sure I wanted to be a part of, I couldn't. I couldn't hate him. There was more purpose in my life than I ever had before. There was more meaning in life than I had ever experienced living quietly on the farm. He gave me something to fight for, something to aspire to be. That was something I could not fault him for. I was glad he was in my life, glad he made me mad, giddy, laugh and cry. I would take all of it again, everything that had happened to us, as long as it led me to him.

"No." His voice was quiet. "It's not odd, it's comforting actually." His tail curled around us. "To know you feel this way too." We met each other's gaze, and something passed between us. Something almost tangible. I shivered, not out of fear, but from an emotion I could only imagine before. Was this what it was like to *want* someone?

I wanted Shroding, and a small part of me, the rational part, the part with good sense and preservation, cried out a warning that if I went there, if I loved Shroding, as Mama Meod had so blatantly pointed out, I would not recover from it if he broke my heart.

I gazed into his onyx eyes, seeing them with unnerving clarity. He leaned in, pressing his furred forehead to mine in a way that spoke of trust and friendship. I reminded myself that even if this hurt later, I would let myself love Shroding regardless of the end.

"Good night," I whispered, rubbing him behind the ears and letting his purr coax me to sleep.

"See you soon." He nodded his ears, twitching back as he pulled away.

I watched him turn in a circle, settling into a silver ball at the crook of my knees, and did my best not to think about tomorrow and how I was going to convince Callum to trust me.

CHAPTER 22
A Way Out

After I woke up, Shroding asked to go on a walk around the village with me. The sun was bright, reflecting off the snow-laden ground. People bustled about, as productive as any city might be.

"How did you end up in the lake?" Shroding asked after we had walked a ways.

Glad he was finally saying something, I explained that Miles had followed us and attacked our camp.

"I was running away and lost my footing near the cliff edge above the water." I looked out at the vast lake before us. "Then Callum saved me." I yawned, still half-asleep as we trekked through the snow. "What do you think happened to Miles?"

"I wish I knew," Shroding said bitterly, and it sounded more like, "If I did, he would be dead."

"So how did you get here this time?"

"I was brought here by Lev and a few other warriors. They found me in the gully."

I sighed. "Well, I suppose it's a good thing they brought us both to the same place."

He nodded.

"Miles said something odd when he found me. He said someone was looking for me, wanted to meet me. From my experience with him and the marauders, I figured meeting whoever that was wouldn't be a good thing, which is why I ran. Do you have any idea who it could be?"

"Not in the least."

"It seemed like he knew I had the king's power."

"Then it's good you ran, even though you nearly died." But his words sounded different, like instead he was saying, "I'm sorry I couldn't protect you." Was I reading too much into his unspoken words? Was this how it would be between us now? A line crossed, and we couldn't go back. Tension simmered between us. Me wanting something he refused to give, to the point that I guilted him into giving it to me. I should free him from the oath, but... I wouldn't.

"I made fire, on my own." I pushed my shoulders back, recalling how excited and proud I'd been, how badly I'd wanted to tell him.

"Really?" He shifted to face me. "That's excellent!" The delight in his tone was better than any words of compliment he could have given. Bolstered, I walked closer to him.

"I know! I just did all the things we practiced, and then bam!" I wiggled my fingers like flames. "I can use the power to save you, just wait."

"You have come a long way. Your control and focus is progressing nicely, but making me human again is going to be... complicated," he said with humor.

"A lot of things with you are complicated," I teased, but regretted it when he looked away.

"The fighters here are some of the best I've seen. It would be good to learn what you can from them while we are here."

I tucked my chin. The moment had passed. "Of course."

"Do you know what Coinania is?" he asked after a moment.

"The name of this place?" I shrugged.

"Yes, but it is more than that. Look…"

We had walked up to a high point in the village, one that overlooked the homes below.

I peered down at the people and tents.

"They live as a unit, as a team. See that man who is carrying two rabbits?"

I glanced around till I found the man in question. He looked similar to Lev. He called to the entrance of another tent and gave the rabbits to a young boy no more than six or seven.

"I don't understand, what am I seeing?" I rubbed my eyes.

"That boy's father is sick. His father or mother would have done the hunting, but his mother is pregnant and can't. That man, while hunting for his own family, procured food for them without being asked. The family who received the rabbits didn't doubt that they would have food to eat today. They trusted their community, just as their community saw their need and offered to fill it."

"Isn't that just charity?"

"Look at the tent in the center by the firepit."

"I see it." It was the only tent scorched by fire. The frame of the tent was bare like the bones of a corpse.

"Do you see the tent there?" He pointed with his paw to a tent thick with many layers of fabric. A few men and women were stripping off some of the taut layers and rolling them up, hauling them over to the damaged tent. "They have more fabric than they need on their tent, so they are giving the extra to the young couple whose tent caught fire."

"That is kind of them."

"Yes, but it is a kindness gone undemanded and without need for reciprocity. That is Coinania. It is sharing out of a deep knowing that they, as people, own nothing, so they do not feel a defensiveness or a protectiveness over what they have or have not."

I thought about my experiences, how people are jealous and hold the things they have at a greater value than the lives of actual people. I frowned and glanced back at the town.Had my father known of Coinania? Was that why he'd helped the children in our town the way he had? "How can there be a community like this? How can they all behave this way? Someone has to be holding back or harboring bitterness?" I reasoned.

"They all have a commonality. They were all slaves, or would have been if they had stayed in Golan. They have all been set free, and that freedom has united them."

After the tour I looked for Callum but didn't find him anywhere. No one had seen him since the previous night. Adequately deterred, I returned to the tent to sleep, my body aching from being on my feet so long. Though I didn't have a mark on me anymore, my shoulder and leg coursed with pain as if the wounds were still there, hiding under the pristine skin.

"These are your clothes from when we found you," Lev said, laying down the tunic and pants, the older lady from the cabin had given me, on the end table beside the bed.

"Thanks," I acknowledged, rubbing my eyes sleepily.

Whose clothes had I been wearing? Judging from the similar look to Lev's, I assumed they were hers.

"Sorry to wake you again, but dinner is being served." She gestured outside the tent. "It might seem odd, but we do this a few times a week. Get everyone together for dinner; it's kind of our favorite tradition."

I nodded, honored to have been invited to join.

We made our way to the main hall, where dinner would be. I took a seat next to Lev and watched as all the tables filled up with people.

The scent of rosemary and thyme wafted towards my nose. Lev sat on the floor, stirring a small pot over the fire.

"Um, Lev, I've been meaning to ask... if the tent I'm sleeping in is your tent, and I'm using your bed, where have you been sleeping?"

She laughed a little. "My sister's tent, she's next door."

"You have a sister?" I vaguely recalled her saying that a few days ago when I first woke up.

"Half sister, but that's only important when it comes to the line of succession. Her dad was the son of Mama Meod. He passed away a few years back."

"Oh, I'm sorry."

"It's okay." She smiled easily. "I mean, he wasn't my dad."

"So where—" I began to ask about her parents, but she interrupted, misunderstanding my question.

"Your cat's outside."

"Oh?"

"You sure are paranoid about him. Does he run away often or something?"

I frowned, not sure how to bring up the question of her parents again. "Something like that."

"Oh, sounds like a story?" She wiggled her eyebrows expectantly.

"For another time, perhaps," I evaded. "I was looking around for Callum today, I wanted to clear the air between us, but I couldn't find him."

"He comes and goes frequently. I think he said something about going to Tyndale." She tapped her chin in thought. "But for all I know, he could be off to the capital for the Celebration of Strings since that is coming up soon."

"Oh right." I frowned, unsure what to do if I couldn't talk to him.

Food was passed around, and when it got to our table, Lev handed me a bowl of soup. It smelled rich with flavors.

I hesitated for a moment, waiting for her to eat first.

"Dig in!" Lev laughed, shoveling a spoonful into her mouth.

As I ate, a couple people moved to stand at the head of the long table.

"That's Fealth and Marco," Lev said, gulping down the last of her soup and giving her attention to the pair.

"What is it to be a warrior?" a tall man with long dark hair down his back asked. He had bands of ink across the exposed skin of his arms and chest.

A little girl in the front row clapped and with a group of her friends shouted back, "What is it to be a warrior, Fealth?"

Fealth scoffed, snapping his fingers and pointing to the boy next to him. "Marco, tell them." The lean boy with dark hair who looked like a smaller version of Fealth came forward.

"A warrior is to master the gift," he said wisely to the children.

I realized this was all rehearsed as the kids shouted back.

"Krav is the action. It is coordinated movements that those gifted can master to help control the vibrations."

"Without the knowledge of the movements it is impossible to harness vibration in a fight," Fealth finished.

I looked at Lev, who was staring at Marco with a very clear look of adoration. I stifled a smile.

"What are they doing?"

"Teaching." Lev grinned at me, getting to her feet to join the two men.

"And once a warrior is strong enough to harness the gift, then they become protectors of our village. But who do we protect from?" Lev asked, putting her hands on her hips and looking around the room for a threat.

The kids yelled back. "Grieving and Wraiths!"

"How do we stop them?" Fealth yelled, stomping his foot for emphasis.

A boy who looked barely fifteen stood and flipped out a dagger. He charged at Fealth, and I rose from my seat in a panic. Fealth stopped the blade inches from his forehead.

"Grieving, get a headshot!" The young man yelled.

Then Marco moved behind them and pressed his palm into the boy's back, twisting, and he snatched the blade from Fealth and thrust it at the young man's heart.

I nearly screamed, but the blade did not hit flesh.

Mama Meod came up next to me. "Calm, child. They are demonstrating to the children. No one will be hurt."

"I don't understand, is there a way to fight the Wraiths? Wouldn't stabbing them in the heart kill the person?"

"Oh no, no. I forget the rest of the world does not know our secrets." She laughed, and I frowned. Did that mean there was a way to stop possessions?

"You mean there is a way to save someone who is possessed? A way to fight the Wraiths?"

"Yes, yes. It is hard, but get close to the enemy, push out the Wraith using your vibration, and when you do, for just a moment a flaming red heart appears." She flexed her hand in front of her chest. "Pierce it with a blade, and the Wraith will cease to exist."

I stared at her with wide eyes. Why did the world not know this? It would change the tide of the war!

"Go to the arena with Lev and Fealth, they will show you." With that she walked away, leaving me slacked jawed, staring after her.

CHAPTER 23

An Oath Taken

"Teach me how to fight the Wraiths."

Fealth and Lev looked at me, surprised.

"Mama Meod approved this?" Marco asked.

I nodded impatiently.

Lev looked at me like I had lost it, and maybe I had? I felt a little crazy inside. Adrenaline and probably some shock made me jittery. This power would change everything. I would have nothing to fear from the Wraiths anymore.

"I find it hard to believe, with the vibrations coming off you, that you have never used your power to stop a possession before." Fealth's narrowed eyes brought me back to reality.

"It's not something I was taught, I don't think anyone in Shamar is," I defended.

"You would think they would have learned it by now." Lev shook her head sadly. "I can't wrap my mind around it. By the Strings, what is Shamar doing? Do they even want to win the war?"

I shifted uncomfortably. What was she talking about?

"It is odd." Marco approached, analyzing me. Lev's attention diverted to Marco in obvious infatuation.

"It doesn't matter. I want to learn now. So, Fealth, will you teach me, or what?" I demanded.

He grinned and waved me on. We walked to an arena fenced in by hulking pines marred with cuts and patches of broken bark. Clearly the trees took quite a beating.

"Ready?" he warned and with a curt nod began to show me how to move my vibration into another person.

It was unsurprisingly similar to when I shared my power with Shroding.

So I found the technique easy to pick up. Still, I practiced for a while, getting used to pushing my power through another person.

———

The crunch of someone approaching us through the snow had us looking though the pines.

"Callum!" Lev cheered. "You're back?"

He ignored her greeting and made long strides across the snowy arena to me, his gray eyes the color of looming storm clouds. I was tempted to raise my arms and protect myself as his gaze warned of a coming attack. I kept my hands tight to my sides.

I had to convince him of my loyalty to the kingdom and in turn secure his to Shroding.

When he reached me, I fought a flinch as he took my hand in his. "I need to talk with you." Then without another word, I was being pulled from the group and back towards the village.

We passed a few tents, and I was pretty sure I was close

enough now for Shroding to hear me. I told him what was happening and confirmed the clearing by the lake to meet at, just as we'd planned it. At least, this way, if Callum did, somehow, turn out to be the enemy, I would find out before involving Shroding directly.

Now I just needed Callum to follow me.

I glanced at the sky. The sun was sliding down between the mountains in the west. Shroding would be ready to convince him if my words did not.

Callum stopped walking, and I bumped carelessly into his back.

We were between two passageways, a snowdrift so high to the left that the passage was almost completely overtaken. A few wooden boxes and tarps were stacked to the right, and straight ahead was the flap of a tent. Was this Callum's tent? I was about to ask when a man emerged from it.

The man behind Callum came forward and touched Callum's shoulder, signaling him to let me go. Callum did. My hand was instantly cold.

The man's eyes were thin, angular, and an almost out-of-place shade of blue against his thick dark lashes. His hair was cropped short and as sable as raven's feathers. His features were mature and attractive; straight nose, high cheekbones and full lips, fuller than Callum and Shroding's put together. It was positively lethal to have lips that pouty. He had to be in the king's court, as he was another devastatingly glorious man, sent to torture me with his perfection.

He wore the insignia of the king on his belt buckle.

"I can explain everything—" I began, ready to tell the whole sorted tale to Callum and the stranger.

Callum reached to his side, and I was sure we were back

to the dagger-at-my-throat thing, but instead he pulled out a lump of fur.

"Can you explain why this was in your pocket the day I saved you from drowning?"

I looked at the unassuming ball, perplexed. Then the silver strands, like the strings of the vibration gift, wove together, clicking into place.

"You found this in my pocket?" It was the ball of fur I had kept after brushing Shroding at the cabin.

Callum grabbed my wrist and deposited the lump in my palm.

I glanced past the glaring Callum, trying to place the dark-haired man behind him. He was familiar and seemed far more reasonable, helpful even, than Callum.

He tilted his head curiously.

"Asher?" I inferred. A ridiculous smile spread across my features as if I had just solved the world's greatest mystery. He had to be Asher, the piercing blue eyes should have been an obvious clue! However, it wasn't those baby blues that had given him away, it was the way he tilted his head. It was just the way Shroding did when he was waiting for me to figure something out. Shroding had said they were often mistaken for each other when they were little, and even after all this time, their mannerisms were still so exact that it was almost comical.

Asher stiffened. "Yes." His hand moved to the hilt of his sword. "Do you know me? Or are you a spy?" he questioned, joining Callum in an unforgiving glare.

"How do you know the name Shroding?" Callum demanded, bringing my attention back to him.

This was not going well.

These guys were hyperparanoid, and I began to wonder

if maybe this was the real reason why Shroding had hesitated yesterday, not wanting to confront Callum. Maybe it wasn't because he thought they would be the enemy, but instead because he knew they would be distrusting. He wouldn't be able to speak to them like he could me. Perhaps he thought they would misunderstand like they were doing right now; thinking this was some trick.

"... I found Shroding." I internally winced at the shake in my voice, wishing the words had been stronger, more assured.

"I have been with him for weeks, I-I know everything." I realized my confession sounded off. I quickly added, "I'm not a spy, I swear!" My hands lifted in surrender. "I know your names because of Shroding!" My voice was edging towards panic. I needed to calm down. I sounded like a madwoman even to me.

I took a deep breath, my shoulder and chest hating the stretched movement even as I forced another deep breath. How could I get them to believe me?

"You weren't there, but the general, commander, and the court leader were. They saw him get turned into a silver cat..." I trailed off, floundering for more proof. To my surprise, Callum backed away, a smile on his lips. I took another steadying breath. Did they believe me?

"I don't know who you are, but that is quite a story." Callum's smile twisted into a rather dazzling smirk. "A cat? What proof do you have?"

Asher stayed still, hand resting on the sword hilt, waiting.

"T-The moon!" I said with haste. The fur in my hand looked like nothing more than a dust bunny, its amethyst glow not showing at all. "It shines purple in the moonlight!"

Callum and Asher exchanged a look I could not read.

A wave of power left Asher, and I flinched, surprised I

could sense his vibration when I hadn't been able to before. In response, my own power woke up, pricking my fingers as his vibrations rippled through the air around us. I gasped in amazement.

Asher took the fur from my hand.

Callum still held my wrist and gave me a gentle squeeze as Asher lifted the fur. The clear sky was only lit by the stars coming to life above us. For a moment, I marveled at the absurdity of my situation. Tears pricked my eyes, but I forced them back. I needed to find Shroding. Tears could come later. I would feel relief later.

The fur shone silver in the night, the purple hue not visible, as the moon had not taken to the sky yet. Anxiety filled me. How much longer would it take to convince them? For the moon to rise? Shroding was waiting.

"I can take you to him."

Callum's hand tightened around my wrist, and I wondered briefly if his hold was more to keep me from escaping than to stop me from fighting back.

Asher paced, waiting, holding the ball of fur aloft, eyes moving between the stars and his outstretched palm.

Without the moon, would the silver fur be enough proof? Even as the crescent moon tipped over the edge of the tent and bathed us in light, the fur did not change. Why did it not work?

Callum twisted my wrist painfully, about to demand something from the angry slant of his mouth, but Asher gasped, making us both stop and follow his gaze.

The fur remained unchanged, but the sky said everything that needed to be said.

"Callum," Asher breathed.

The brightest star I had ever seen in the night sky gleamed over our heads.

A wash of relief mixed with a strange wonder and bewilderment filled me.

The bright star sat at the top of the constellation Ari, a beloved constellation of a large cat with an empty crown. It was widely known as the king's constellation, one my father had shown me many times. One I would gaze up at with Theo on our dandelion hill night after night. I knew this constellation better than any other in the sky. So I knew the star that sat glowing the brightest at the center of the crown had never been there before.

I was not sure if it was me or Callum who trembled at the very clear sign beaming down at us from the sky. But it hardly seemed to matter, as both men turned to me and demanded in unison, "Where is he?"

CHAPTER 24

Reunited

I led them through the dark to the lake's edge where Shroding and I had decided to meet.

Neither Callum nor Asher spoke to me or asked questions, which I found very odd. One would think they'd be brimming with questions, but we walked in silence.

Their lack of curiosity had me wondering again if they were indeed the enemy somehow and I was leading Shroding into a trap.

We were coming to the edge of the lake, and I knew if Shroding was near he would probably feel the king's power coming from me, and our mental connection would be possible again. I stopped, tugging against Callum's grip on my wrist since he had still not let me go. I first needed to find out if they were on our side or not. I would not endanger Shroding needlessly.

"Why did you stop?" Asher's voice was slightly concerned as he scanned the trees around us. His hand touched the hilt of his sword, prepared for a threat.

Callum looked annoyed but let go of me and moved to

stand next to Asher. Instinctively they both took on an air of protectiveness for each other. Their stance, though casual, positioned them to have each other's back should danger arise. It was not lost on me that I was not included in their protective calculation.

"I need to know." I clenched my first. "Are you trustworthy?"

They raised their eyebrows, glancing at each other, then at me.

"I will not take you to him until I know you mean him no harm. Have you chosen the other side? It has been a long time since you have seen him, and we haven't had much luck with people along the journey so far." I didn't know if a direct approach could be trusted. They could just lie to me. I had no way of knowing if they were really good or not. They did not seem to have vibration sickness, but that wasn't the only dark thing they could have done in the last two hundred years. If they lied, I would have no choice but to believe them. It was futile, my asking, but I had to do something.

Callum spoke first. "You are a fool to think you can ask us and trust what we say." I wanted to snit back that of course I knew.

Asher elbowed him, shaking his head. "Please forgive Callum's rudeness. We just want to see Shroding. If our king no longer has faith in us, then we will leave him or die proving our loyalty." Asher's words seemed sincere. To emphasize his point he put a fist on his chest and gave a deep bow. Still lowered, he continued. "If you need proof of my loyalty I will give it. Please tell me what I can do to assure you."

I licked my lips. I hadn't expected this response. I wasn't sure what he could do to prove his loyalty. Then his bow had me recalling that the king's court was bound by their oaths. Should one break an oath, they would lose their power and be stripped from the king's court. It was no question they were in the court. "Shroding has reason to doubt the loyalty of one of his friends. So I will ask you to swear an oath," I said confidently, lifting my chin.

Callum sputtered something incoherent and looked horrified while Asher kept his head bowed.

"Swear an oath that you have never attempted to kill the prince," I demanded a little forcefully. If they swore it and it was not true, they would lose their power on the spot.

Asher raised his head slightly, eyes suspicious.

"Shroding has been pretty loose-lipped about our laws." Callum sneered.

"What you ask is an oath I can easily swear to you." Asher closed his eyes and took a breath. "I vow I have never attempted to kill the prince, nor will I ever attempt to. You have my oath," he finished strongly, and straightened.

My eyes were wide at the addition Asher had made to the oath. I silently reprimanded myself for not thinking of it.

I wasn't sure what should happen if he'd lied—Asher crumpling to the ground, burning for his lie, succumbing to instant death—but when nothing happened, it seemed safe to say Asher was on our side.

Callum watched, a sick look on his face. "I cannot believe I am doing this right now..." He whined.

I waited warily. Callum was a hot-tempered type and didn't seem to like me much.

"You know, lass, that if this wasn't for our king, I would never in my hundreds of years swear an oath to you." He scoffed, appraising me with clear contempt. Asher elbowed him again. "Fine, fine." Callum huffed, put his fist to his chest as Asher had done, and lowered his head slightly. "I have never attempted to kill the prince, nor will I ever attempt to. You have my oath." Again, nothing happened, and I wondered if I had done something wrong.

Since there was not much else I could do to verify their intentions, I nodded, assuming they were steadfast in their commitment to the prince.

"Okay," I whispered, and led on.

When we arrived at the edge of the tree line, I spotted Shroding with his back to us. I knew he could sense me and the others I was with. He paced back and forth under a large oak that had thick enough branches to protect him from the present moonlight.

Catching the sound of our approach, he stopped and turned, crouching low into the shadows. My relief flooded our connection, and I knew he could feel how my emotions swelled at the sight of him. This was it. The moment everything changed for us. It would no longer be just Shroding and me. Us against the power of Skithian. Us trying to bring him back to his human form, and us trying to save the world.

His iridescent eyes turned to me.

"Haya," Shroding breathed shakily in my mind. It was a mix of relief and concern.

"Shroding..." I said to him in my mind. We looked at each other for a moment, our eyes locked, communicating mutual fear and hope. Our mutual loss of this strange time we had shared together.

"Asher and Callum are here," I said calmly, a nervous pit in my stomach as I pointed to what he could clearly see.

Callum and Asher stared at Shroding, who emerged slowly from under the tree. His eyes flickered iridescent in the light, and I swallowed the lump in my throat as his fur gradually shifted as the curtain of moonlight transformed his silver fur to a rich amethyst.

To all our surprise, Asher bounded forward, to snatch Shroding into his arms. Amazingly Asher was able to lift Shroding, though it looked like he struggled a bit.

I tried not to laugh at the alarmed strangled meow Shroding let out.

"What the— What are you doing? Put me down! Asher! Put me down right now!" Shroding hollered in my mind, and, like a string snapping, the tension disappeared. I laughed out loud, grabbing my stomach and doubling over. I laughed harder when everyone looked at me perturbed.

"He..." I gasped between fits, "would like you," I wheezed, "to put him down." I wiped tears from my eyes.

"It's not funny," Shroding growled, and I suppressed another outburst of laughter, sure I had finally lost it. After everything that had happened, I had cracked. I sniffled and slowly limped to Asher, my body aching after the training and long walk to the lake.

Callum watched me cautiously, following silently at my side.

Asher's eyes danced from me to Shroding and back and then to Callum. "I can't believe any of this," he wondered with a goofy smile on his face that made him look as youthful as Lev. Putting Shroding on the ground, he continued, "I never thought, I never dreamed, but by the Strings I had hoped, I had prayed..." He trailed off, words incoherent. I understood his relief as the knot in my own chest unraveled.

"Shroding?" Callum said in awe. Hesitantly he knelt to be eye level with his king. I could only assume it was disorienting seeing his friend, his king, as a cat. Slowly, as slowly as I had on the dandelion hill, Callum reached out to touch Shroding's fur. Shroding with equal hesitation brought his head to meet Callum's hand.

"Brother."

It was so faint, but I heard it. The reverence in Shroding's tone sent a shiver down my spine. Shroding respected Callum, the way a son might regard a father. The way I had regarded Theo. I lowered my eyes. Something about the moment was too intimate and tender. I could feel the honor and adoration they had for one another.

It was beautiful.

Callum's face shifted through so many emotions, but when it finally landed on a reluctant smirk, he lifted his hand to gently scratch Shroding behind the ear. He was obviously teasing him. Without missing a beat, Shroding nipped at Callum's hand and jumped onto his shoulder. Callum faltered, tumbling over, the weight making him lopsided. He rolled onto the ground and laughed. It was deep and hearty, with a softness I couldn't have imagined Callum having. Callum's laugh sounded so much like Theo's that my heart ached.

Tears pricked my eyes, but I steadied a happy smile at Shroding so he would not worry. He had been alone for so long, and now I was watching friends, separated for two hundred years, reunite in joy and laughter. It was tears of my own joy that poured from me now, knowing this reunion was only the beginning for Shroding. Only the beginning of his return to the life he had thought was lost forever.

———

Shroding and I had considered the inevitability of him needing to communicate with others when I was not around. So we had constructed a simple board and wooden blocks with all the letters needed for him to write. It was time consuming, but it was the best option we could think of under such a time constraint.

I explained to Asher and Callum how it worked and let them know when I was around I would be happy to translate, since I had the king's power.

That tidbit did not even seem to faze either of them. I supposed they must have gathered that I had the king's power.

So with their oath in my heart and the joy in Shroding's eyes, I left them to reconnect.

It wasn't my place to interfere with the reunion. When they were ready to leave for Tyndale, they would let me know.

I trudged through the snow and returned to the arena to continue training.

Lev and the others were all panting and lying down like they had just run up the side of the mountain.

"What did I miss?"

"Haya! I was about to hunt you down, sure Callum had gone and done something stupid again."

I shrugged noncommittally. "He had a moment of no stupidity for once," I joked, earning a delighted laugh from her.

"Now you're getting it."

I looked up towards the village; the sky glowed a strange amber, and the smell of smoke filled the arena.

CHAPTER 25

Nephesh Maveth

A scream rattled through the night, making the hair on my arms rise and everyone sprint from the arena to the village.

"What's happening?" I floundered, eyes rolling over children running towards the arena. People scattered all around to put out the fires.

Gone was the silly young girl who had been joking with me moments ago.

Lev yelled at the kids, "This way, into the bunker! You know the drill!"

Fealth and Marco plucked children from the hillside and deposited them into a hatch on the far side of the training ground.

I stood and watched, bewildered.

"Haya, get down to the lake. We will handle this and let you know when it's safe," Lev ordered, shaking me from my confusion.

"What's happening?" I asked again.

"The Wraiths are here. They are attacking. The kids will

be safe in the bunker from those of us who get possessed. Now go." She shoved me in the direction of the water.

The Wraiths were here? They'd found us? They were possessing the people of Coinania? Was Shroding safe? I tried to reach him with my mind, but we were too far from each other.

I clenched my fists. I did not have to be afraid anymore. I could fight them just like the rest of them.

"No, I will stay."

Lev appraised me for only a moment, then tossed me a short knife. "Remember to aim for the flaming heart after you push the Wraith out."

The blade was cold and heavy in my hand. *Strings, don't let me accidentally kill anyone.*

"Lev!"

We turned to see Fealth convulsing on the ground, a child pinned down and crying under his weight.

"Fealth, what are you—" A slap like the vibration of thunder tossed me across the snow. My lower back connected with a tree, halting the momentum and shaking the fresh fall of white in clumps from the branches. I gasped, coughing and wiping ice from my face.

When my eyes focused, Lev had freed the child, closing the latch to the bunker, but Fealth's eyes pulsed violet in the dark, focused solely on me.

I got to my feet, drawing out the king's power.

Lev was jumped by a woman who had been chasing one of the children Lev had saved. She couldn't help me.

I had to save Fealth myself.

"Fealth, you have to be in there somewhere, you don't want to hurt me," I said, breathless, trying to buy time. The knife was in the snow a few paces away. I looked around for anything I could fight back with. Quickly I made a snowball and threw it at his face. With unnatural ease he tilted his head, avoiding my strike, but it gave me a moment to dive for the dagger.

I fumbled in the snow and forced the king's power to fill me faster than any other time before. It flooded my veins, a torrent I welcomed.

I could do this.

The Wraith came at me, throwing wave after wave, shattering trees on all sides. I pulled power into my limbs, dodging as best I could and getting hit with the aftershocks, as I wasn't fast enough. My control was sloppy. I was not used to doing so many things at once with the power.

I had to get close enough to him. Invisible strings corded around my arms, holding me back.

I thrashed to get free, but Fealth charged me, blurring before stopping in front of me, freezing fingers closing over my throat. Air burned to get down the passageway. My chest squeezed painfully with fear.

I closed my eyes, tallying my breaths. Even if these were my last ones, I would make them count. I would not let Fealth be used by the Wraith to hurt anyone else. The bands holding my arms slackened, and I pressed my palms to his chest.

Falling into the vibration dimension was easier than other times, maybe because I was dying, the barrier between the dimensions weaker somehow? Whatever the reason, I could see Fealth's Nephesh, the way his strings were clamped down by darkness. A darkness different from the black of the vibration dimension. At the center was a sticky mass that pulsed a dead song, like nothing my ears had ever heard before. I felt sick at the sound, as if it could poison me just by hearing it.

I imagined Shroding's melody and focused on that frequency instead of the song that resonated from the dark mass. When I locked onto it, I pushed my power straight through, letting the friction ignite.

The pressure on my throat eased, and when I opened my eyes, I could see it. The flaming heart hovering just outside Fealth's chest.

The knife was slippery in my hand, but I clutched it with all my strength and drove it into the heart of the Wraith.

A screech just like the terrible song burned through my ears, bringing tears to my eyes, as the monster withered and died.

Fealth collapsed as Lev ran over. "You did it!" she cheered, but I did not feel joy or relief. Though it was a monster, though it had been trying to kill me, it had once been a man, a soldier, someone's friend, child, and now its soul was gone forever.

Bile stuck in my throat.

Lev did not seem to understand my silence as she hauled me up to my feet.

"The village needs us." She kicked Fealth's side. "Hey, get up, we have work to do."

Fealth grunted, rousing, and after a quick glance at us, he understood what had happened. He turned his caramel eyes to me.

"Thanks."

Still I said nothing, but I ran with them to the town.

Fire, ash... ruin again.. The glowing eyes of the Wraiths flickered, and my chest twisted and rolled with sharp anxiety.

All was falling apart again. I'd done this, I'd brought them here! Now Lev's home would be destroyed just like mine...

"Where is Mama Meod?" I called, watching the possessed attack their friends and family.

"She has a bunker of her own. None of us could save her if she gets possessed, she is too strong."

"I thought they didn't come here 'cause they are afraid of her?"

"They are not afraid of her but of the knowledge we possess to eradicate them." Fealth howled as he charged into the fray, taking out a Wraith infinitely faster than I could. I would only be a burden if I stayed to fight.

"Lev, I—"

"Yes, go find your cat." She waved me off, running into the chaos.

I turned to go to the lake; I would help anyone I found along the way.

A woman ran up to me, eyes unmarred by a purple glow but frantic all the same.

"Commander Callum needs you, he's in the chief's tent. He said it's urgent!"

Before I could ask anything else, she was gone, screaming as she ran, as if Wraiths chased her very steps. I didn't have energy to spare for her. Callum had been with Shroding last —did that mean Shroding was in trouble?

I volleyed through the maze of tents, amazed at how quickly the Wraiths were falling to the people of Coinania. These may be simple folk, but they were warriors.

The chief's tent was in the center of the village, not accessible by any of the pathways.

"Callum?" I called uncertainly, taking a small step into

the tent. The tent was dark compared to the fires lighting the sky outside. My eyes struggled to adjust.

A single lantern lit the far corner. He stood, his back to me, the hood of a cloak pulled over his head.

He shifted at my presence, waving me to move deeper into the space, beckoning me over to him.

"Where is Shroding? What happened?" I rambled, looking around for my silver friend.

His hood shifted, the light of the lantern casting the faintest glow on his profile.

My brow furrowed, dismay filling me.

His shoulders rose and fell in a deep inhale. "That scent." He spoke, but his voice was low, scratchy and nothing like the snarky, brooding commander I had gotten to know.

"Who—?"

The strange man laughed, an awful, sinister sound that ghosted over my skin in a familiar way. "The king's power, I smell it all over you."

"Who are you?" I raised my fists to fight, making my way slowly between the shelves. "Show yourself," I demanded.

"That's no way to greet a guest." Impossibly he vanished, and then arms snaked around my waist.

My hair tumbled over my shoulder as my braid came loose. "That's better." The voice slithered in my ear. The voice from my memory. The voice from ten years ago was as clear as day. I shoved free from his hold, turning on him, fist raised in a Krav stance.

"Logan," I demanded shakily.

"My, my, she is clever after all." His face was still shadowed as he moved in, corralling me like he had when I was just a child. He grinned deviously as I staggered back into the stone fireplace at the center of the tent; the rough face pressed painfully into my back and arms.

I drew my power, but in a blur his fist connected with my gut, making the tent spin. I gasped, the air wrenched from me as I doubled over. There was no time to scream, let alone fight back, before he was on me, forcing me to the ground with his body weight. I couldn't move. He had completely immobilized me. When I could breathe again, I tried to call air to fill my lungs, but my breaths were panicked, too shallow and racing. His knees pinned my thighs, digging in so hard, tears pricked my eyes. His large hands crushed my shoulders as I clawed at his forearms, desperate to get free.

"Your father's name—Armond Golden, like your great-great-grandfather, yes?" Logan asked, leaning down close enough for me to see his face in the flickering lights. He was a slightly older version of the boy from the alley. His eyes were pure yellow, thin vertical pupils making him look inhuman. He knelt, his face inches from mine. "I have a secret," he whispered, reaching up to unbutton the top of his shirt, and pulled it aside to reveal a long gnarled scar just above his collarbone, down across his heart. "Your father was the one who gave me this scar."

My eyes went wide, and I trembled.

"We met on the battlefield twenty years ago, except he didn't know what I was. He fought hard." He grinned wolfishly, and my mind went to the limp my father had my whole life. From a battle fought years before my birth. "I fought harder," he seethed, letting go of his collar, his shirt hanging loose under the cloak. "I have many reasons to hate you. You," he said with a sneer licking his lips, "who would bring Shroding back. You, the daughter of the man who scarred me. You, who unconsciously replicate the court with your braid. You, who try so hard to be something you are not. Just. Like. Me." His fingernails dragged up the side of my neck, twisting around to my nape and scraping painfully up into my scalp before splaying out. It could have been a tender way to cradle one's head, if not for the way his nails cut across the sensitive skin, drawing blood.

He fisted my hair, pulling so my chin jutted out to the side. Teeth flashed in my peripheral as he leaned down, his hot breath trailed over my skin, nose inhaling as it traveled along my jaw.

His tongue dragged along my pulse before the curling pain and pressure of his teeth cut into the base of my neck, breaking through skin. I finally had enough air to scream, but it was muffled by his hand a second later. His palm covered my nose and mouth as his face pressed into the curve of my throat. Had Logan just bitten me? A blast of vibration, whose I couldn't be sure, sparked the lantern, the flame bursting white before flickering sporadically, casting the tent into deranged chaos. Blood slid down my collar.

He moaned, its vibration rippling against my chest.

I froze, my whole body going cold.

Something foreign, dark, was seeping into my blood where his teeth had penetrated. He moaned again, and the sound traveled into my body through my open skin at his lips. I whimpered against his hand. Tears streamed down my face into my ears. It was hard to breathe, and nausea knotted in my stomach as he continued to moan what could have almost been words if his lips were not firm against my pulse.

My vision swam as warm blood matted my hair and soaked into my clothes.

With a grunt, he pulled back and smiled, my blood slotted between his teeth.

He laughed a dark, satisfied chuckle.

"You have no power against me now."

I called on the king's power, but I couldn't feel it—nothing, it was gone. I could not fight back; whatever he had done to me was blocking my access to the gift.

"What did you do?" I wheezed.

"Don't die on me just yet," he whispered, taking my hand and pressing it against the wound as if to staunch the flow. "I still need to draw out the king's power from you." He shifted his weight, pulling a dagger from his side along with a yellow journal.

My eyes focused even as I fought the urge to throw up and pass out. This monster had one of the king's journals? How?

He opened the book and placed it next to my head. He pulled my hand from my neck and splayed my blood-covered palm upwards. He took a deep inhale. The smell of blood and dirt hung in the air, making my head spin.

All thoughts left me as the silver dagger glinted in the lantern light, poised over my body.

I was going to die.

I would never get the chance to save Shroding. He would be trapped forever as a cat, unable to save our world and become everything he is supposed to be.

I wheezed as I once more tried to reach for the king's power inside me, to fight back.

Shroding...

"Haya!" Voices called close by, maybe even just outside the tent.

"Till we meet again, you helpless thing," the man cursed, lifting off me in a blur and vanishing into the shadows of the tent.

My consciousness drifted in and out. I don't know how long I lay there, bleeding, drifting.

I felt their arms before I saw them. Callum was pulling a blanket over me.

Lev cradled my head in her lap. Fabric pressed to my throat.

"Haya, Haya..." Lev breathed, seeing me come to. "What happened?" My eyes focused; the scattered light of the lantern was replaced by the bright warmth of a fire in the hearth.

"Shroding?" I begged as I tried to remember. What *had* happened?

"He is safe," Callum assured me. I cringed as the fabric on my neck was peeled away. "What manner of beast bit you?" Callum demanded so ferociously that I would have flinched had I not been so weak.

The memory was fuzzy like a dream, but I was sure of one thing. "Logan," I breathed. I was tired, my limbs like the stone of the mountains, immovable and cold, so very cold.

Callum stilled, his hands pausing in their effort to bandage my neck.

Mama Meod came along my other side. "This is Nephesh Maveth."

"Soul death?" Lev whispered.

"Save. Her," Callum bit out.

How odd, I didn't think he liked me. Then again Shroding needed me, no... the king's power. A power I could not reach.

"I can only heal the wound so much, I cannot stop it from taking her life."

"No..." Lev cried, her tears falling onto my cheek.

I closed my eyes.

I just wanted to see him.

Just one more time.

THE STORY WILL CONTINUE IN...
From Sapphire Oceans

Shroding's POV
Jealousy

"Haya, I'm coming back to camp."

The tremble that coursed through my limbs was not my own. She was afraid. I had to get to her.

I leapt from rock to rock, the drizzle making the stones slippery. Still I bounded towards her, determined.

Even after my foot slipped and cut against craggy thorns growing between the rocks, even after two of my claws ripped as I volleyed to a high ledge. My chest heaved, injuries all but forgotten by the weight of her panic. My heart hammered in time with hers.

I reached out in my mind, desperate to comfort, to assure her I was coming, but I could not tell if she heard me.

Was it the wolves, Callum, something worse? Had I miscalculated how quickly the Grieving could catch up? Were there more marauders in the woods?

Strings. I should not have gone so far from her, knowing how injured she was.

The canteen stung across my torso, rubbed against my stitched chest. The burn was nothing compared to the burn of her terror that lived in every particle of my being. I would never get used to feeling her emotions. They were all-consuming. Filling me, shaping me, polluting my mind and thoughts. It was miserable. It was wonderful. I had begun to both crave and loathe them. The latter especially now. Especially when I was not there to abate her fear.

The sky split, and a deluge of rain and hail plummeted to the ground like a torrent of freezing knives. The hail was the size of a quenton coin, near the size of my paw. I dodged them as best I could. As they hit the rocks, they burst, shattering. One crashed in front of me, and I lifted my paw to shield myself from the ice shards. Another slammed into my back, rolling off and clanking to the stones. The thunderous rumble of each ice chunk falling filled the gully, making it impossible to hear the flood of water cascading down from the glacier above.

I climbed, desperate to get free of the water trap. I had always been so careful, never getting too close to rivers or streams. Avoiding large bodies of water, wary of getting too close. My density was the one thing I could not protect myself from. If I fell into any body of water, I would drown. I would sink to the bottom with no way out. I had almost died that way in the early years of being a cat, and I'd sought out that end only a few weeks ago, when I had given up hope. When I had wished for death and almost took it for myself, before her. Before Haya and her bright eyes and sweet smile. Before the hope she had returned to me.

I could still feel her body trembling, still taste her distress.

I grunted in pain, my stitches stretching and scraping against the rocks as I hoisted myself up, the water level rising faster than I could climb. My own alarm mixed with hers till I was not sure where hers ended and mine began.

I had to escape the flood. But I wouldn't be able to.

Water lapped at my hind legs, and my paws scrambled for purchase.

I would lose her, and as water drenched the fur of my backside, I knew this time I would not find her.

Strings, how could it end this way?

Images flashed in my mind. Trees blurred past her as she ran. Miles yelled after her.

Miles, that monster, had followed us? Ire, white hot, lit in my core. If I had my powers, he would have burned to dust the moment he laid a hand on her. But I didn't have my powers, and so he had lived and found us.

I roared in frustration. Freezing water wrapped around me on all sides. I could not escape; there was nothing for me to grapple on to, and the closest branch to leap to was a greater jump than I could manage without something for my hind legs to push off.

The current was aggressive as it slammed me into the mud and stone my front claws clung to.

More images poured through my mind.

Haya was falling, a massive body of water stretched out before her, a thin layer of ice overtop.

The sensation of falling, the crash of water wrapped around her as it was me.

"Swim," my mind ordered. "Swim, Haya," I demanded.

The shock of the cold disoriented her, and she thrashed, trying to find her way up. Desperation like my own hammered around inside me.

The defining crack of ice and water erupted around her. She was swallowed up in seconds, the gray sky of the day blotted out by waves of dark water. A sharp burning scratched my chest as she rolled through the water, lost in the twists and turns. She screamed in pain, her shoulder resisting her attempts to move it, and her injured leg refused to kick.

She was drowning, much as I would be in a few moments myself.

"Haya," I pleaded, needing her to live. Needing her to swim to the surface, needing one of us to survive.

The image of my human face filled her mind. I had not recognized my own face the first time she thought of me. I had assumed she was thinking of another boy she liked. It had confused me, why that image of the same man filled her thoughts when I was around, until one day it clicked. The face she imagined all those times was mine. I was surprised by how different I looked. It had been over two hundred years, and I did not look like the thirteen-year-old boy I had been. I had grown up to look a lot like my father. The shape of my face, the build of my body—all his. It was then I realized how attractive I had become. Still, I was certain I could not look as mystical as she thought I was. A glow of light always surrounded my face when she thought of me. Even in cat form, she always thought of me with light, golden or amethyst, encompassing my form. As if I were the sun itself. She thought of my face frequently, and I'd liked it, much more than I ever should.

Now I loathed her seeing my face, even as warmth spread through her at the thought of me, because I knew she was giving up. Resigning herself to drown, and her final thoughts were of me.

I cried out, the roar loud and shaking with all my anger. I would lose her too; I would lose her and then my own life.

She pictured my jaw, dark curls and eyes, a look in them I

recognized instantly. The look I was pretty sure I gave her often. A look I was positive she did not understand.

Her thoughts turned to despair that she could not save me. That she could not help bring me back. I would not become king. But she did not know it wasn't just her drowning that would prevent that. My own watery grave splashed over my face, trying to take me under.

Icy water penetrated our lungs. I would die twice. I would feel her die first, and then only after I knew she was truly gone would I let myself go. I owed her at least that much. Because of me, she'd lost everything. A chance at marriage, her family, her home, and worst of all, her innocence. The smile she'd worn when she first met me was still bright, though she'd worried for her family and was burdened with the responsibility of the farm. Her smile after the night of the fire was a ghost of what it once was, and it was all because of me. I'd ruined her life, and now she would lose it.

Water filled my nose as Haya thrashed, air escaping her mouth in a burst of bubbles. Her thoughts screamed for someone to help her. Disgust twisted in my stomach, her pleas like a knife to my chest, well deserved and not nearly agonizing enough. I deserved this. Deserved to feel her last breath. Maybe that was why the king's power had linked us, not only so I could feel and protect her, but so when I failed to do so, the grief and disgrace would destroy me twice over.

The burning in her chest intensified as her mind slipped away. I would die hating myself for losing her. Hating what I had done. Hating my father and Skithian, everything and everyone who had brought us to this end.

Even as rancor shadowed my mind, her peace and resignation floated through me.

"Haya," I whispered as the surface slipped farther away from us both. I could no longer feel her, sense her. She was gone.

A yawning emptiness overtook my own drive to live. I did not paddle—it would not help if I did. I would sink. Water was my end as I'd feared it would be after the first near-death experience all those years ago.

The silence in me was deafening, as I had no time to even mourn the loss of the hope she had given me. Mourn her.

Bubbles left my lips as I sank, my last thought of her tentative smile as she twisted the end of her braid draped over her shoulder.

Haya...

————

The sensation of being tangled, bound and tied, woke me. I hissed and growled as my captors dragged me on a tarp behind them.

"He's awake," a woman with dark hair bound at the nape of her neck said. Three others were with her. A young girl— maybe the older one's sister, judging from the similar facial structure—and two men. I clawed to get out of the net.

I had survived, and Haya...

Haya...

What had happened to her? Was she really gone?

Yes, she was.

I had felt her die.

I bared my fangs and whimpered, giving up the fight to escape.

"It's okay, kitty, we saved you. You will be alright." The young girl smiled, eyes kind. Perhaps these people did not mean me harm? If that were true, then why was I bound?

What did it matter anyway?

The girl reached down tentatively. When her hands brushed through my fur, I did not purr. I did not respond. Her touch was not Haya's. It did not cause in me the stir Haya's smile and strokes did.

"There, there," she cooed. "We will let you out once we are back home. You're injured."

Oh right. The stitches. They'd opened in my desperate attempts to get out of the gully.

"Quit talking to it, Lev. It doesn't understand," one of the men said.

The other grunted as he hauled me along the path. "One heavy beast he is."

"Fealth, he's clearly scared," Lev chided. "I'm trying to reassure him."

The girl was kindhearted, but she was wrong. Fear was not what I felt.

It was more like desolation.

"Leave him be, Lev," the older girl ordered, and though Lev looked displeased, she listened, moving to walk ahead with the rest.

If I had been paying better attention, I would have noticed who they were and where they were taking me.

"It's been a long time, my furry friend."

I looked up at the old lady before me. The smell of her skin was familiar. I had been in such a stupor since being hauled up from my watery prison. This village was one I had come to many years ago. The old lady before me was once a young girl, bright and beaming like the girl, Lev, who had brought me to the tent I lay in now.

"Do you remember me?" the lady asked.

It was an easy yes. In her youth, when I had come here, she had told me tales of a coming king. They were tales to her, but I knew them to be true. In fact, I'd stayed in this place longer than any other in my last two hundred years as a cat because these people believed in a coming king. They believed a prince had indeed been born. I was naive then. I had believed I could stay with these people. Live out my days in the mountains alongside them. But much like it had happened with Haya, the night I'd revealed my glowing fur to the woman, the first night I had let anyone see the moonlight touch my fur, the Wraiths had come, and the village had been possessed and destroyed. I had believed they all perished. But the girl I had known then had grown into this old woman.

I nodded at her, resting my face in her outstretched palm.

"I'm glad you are alive. I never stopped wondering what happened to you." She rubbed behind my ears. "I lost many that day. I even became next in line for chieftain. My name was lost as I became the leader of these people. Mama Meod, they call me now." She chuckled softly as if she had been waiting years to tell me these things. Perhaps she had.

I didn't have the energy nor desire to purr for her, as I had in the past. I was still alive, despite all the times I could have and almost had died. I had again outlived another person who had become important to me.

Turning away from her hand, I lay back down and closed my eyes. Nothing mattered now. Even seeing this old friend again was little comfort because, like everyone I would get close to, they perished prematurely or with age. She was just another to be taken from me soon enough.

"You have been through some hardships since we parted." Her voice shook, and slowly she traced the stitches along my skin. I vaguely wondered how much blood I needed to lose to actually die.

"I didn't have the gift when we met before, I was too young." Her hands cradled my stomach, and though her body trembled from her old age, her hands were as steady as a practiced surgeon.

Before I registered what she was doing, the air was pushed out of me in a forceful but not painful whoosh.

My wounds began to mend.

She had become a healer? What a marvelous gift. Such a perfect power for the kindhearted, sweet girl she had been and clearly still was.

As she worked on me, my breathing became easier, and all but the pain in my heart subsided.

"Oh Strings," the lady gasped as the final wound faded from my skin. "You are more than you appear."

My eyes shot open. What did she mean? Could she— Yes, she very well could know who I was because I had foolishly forgotten the one thing that made healing so dangerous.

While healing, the healer's gift mingles with the wounded ones' Nephesh, their soul. When this happens, the healer can see the most critical memories from that person's life. The memories that shaped them at their core. Regardless of whether the injured person has the vibration gift, the healer can always see these visions. A physical wound can damage the soul, so it is the only way to truly heal someone. However, even after the injury is mended, the pain remains because the mind cannot be tricked into believing it is unharmed when it knows it had been. I never thought, never even considered that healing me would work the same as a human.

Had she seen my memories? Did she know I was the prince trapped in the body of a cat?

"A few weeks ago I saw something peculiar soar across the night sky." She rose, joints cracking as she shuffled over to a desk on the other side of the room. I watched her eyes, sharp for any sign of malintent. She opened a drawer and pulled out a small yellow leather-bound book.

She presented it to me.

It was one of my father's journals, similar to the one Haya had.

Mama Meod recited a passage:

"The king's power has been found,
The lost king shall abound.
The light of night tells of warning and anticipation,
As royal streaks in cloudless sky confound;
So begins the end of mourning and segregation."

She tapped the book. "These are the words of the king. I think a part of me knew, even when I was just a girl, how important you are."

I sprang to my feet, crouching low, looking for the moment where this pleasant reunion took a dark turn.

"The girl you seek now is close by. Two tents down." She smiled, eyes vanishing behind wrinkles as she waved her hand dismissively. "Nothing more need be said between us."

I shuffled back a step. Haya? Did she mean Haya? Was she alive? Impossible.

I shook my head, but my heart hammered hopefully as I ran through the tent flap, down the corridors, glad they had rebuilt the village the same as it had been before the Wraiths had ruined it all.

I ran at a breakneck speed.

Without a second thought, I was in the tent Mama Meod had told me to go to.

Lev sat on a stool next to a cot. Long hair hung over the edge of the bed.

I leapt to the side of the person lying down and receiving Lev's careful attention.

Eyes closed, lips parted, and chest rising and falling was Haya. She *was* alive.

Strings, she was somehow still alive.

I collapsed next to her, desperate to reach her mind, blinded by my relief and disbelief.

"Hey, kitty, do you know this girl?"

I purred senselessly, curling tightly to Haya's side.

"Callum found her drowning. He seemed to know her as well. He should be back any second."

I didn't want to leave her, not ever again... but Callum. He had saved her twice now—could I trust him? No, I wasn't ready, not yet. I was not really sure of him.

My ears perked at the thump of heavy footsteps Lev had not noticed yet. With a hiss I dropped to the floor and hid behind barrels of what smelled like salt and wine.

"How is she fairing?" Callum's deep voice filled the small tent.

"Breathing, thanks to you."

"She has not woken?"

"Not yet. Mama Meod healed her the best she could, but now it's up to the girl. We are keeping her as warm as possible. The damage from hypothermia has been avoided, but her body is still cold. A fever is growing. The next few hours will be the test."

I peered through the small gap between the barrels to see them.

Callum rubbed his jaw in a more mature version of the gesture he'd used as a kid. In place of his commander's uniform he wore similar clothes to the people of the mountains. Thick sweaters and furs.

"Did you..." Callum lifted the hem of Haya's shirt in question, "dress her in these?" I bit back a snarl at the casual way he touched her.

"Of course, her clothes were soaked. Even though you were smart to get her changed so quickly on the shore, you were drenched as well, and by the time you got her here, the back of your sodden clothes had her all wet again." Lev wasn't scolding but matter-of-fact, as if saying "What did you think would happen?"

"Ah, of course."

"Glad to see you are all changed as well. You should have Mama Meod check you over just to be sure you don't get sick."

He waved her off. "I'll be fine, healthy as a horse."

Lev rolled her eyes. "She won't use her gift. You know how much she loathes doing so."

"That's not—" He sighed as if it was too much energy to explain. "What can we do for her?" He looked down at Haya.

"Keep her as warm as possible." To enforce her point, Lev rolled a thick fur overtop of her. "I need to go talk with my sister. Can you keep an eye on her?"

Callum continued to stare down at Haya, as if he had not heard Lev at all.

"Callum?" Lev prompted.

"Hm?" Callum looked up, and my stomach rolled at the chagrin on his face. As if he'd been caught doing something he ought not to.

Lev raised a speculative brow. "You know her, don't you?"

"Sort of."

Lev's eyes turned playful. "I'm only saying this because I'm pretty sure she will be okay, but judging from the state of her ribs when you brought her in, you gave her mouth-to-mouth, didn't you." She winked cheekily at him.

Callum scowled. "She was dying."

"Mhm, so you can honestly say you are not thinking about your mouth on hers, right now?" she goaded.

His jaw ticked as he glanced down at Haya.

"I don't blame you for using that as your first resort. I mean, she is gorgeous."

"It was the only resort. She was dying," he repeated sharply, but he scratched the pad of his thumb with his pointer finger, his tell as a kid when he was embarrassed or lying.

"Callum, how long has it been since you, ya know." She was still playful, but an edge of worry sharpened her words.

"Lev, how old are you?" he said with a tone more warning than question—he knew how old she was. Honestly, I would chastise her too, for asking about a grown man's sex life.

She rolled her eyes. "For someone who has lived as long as you have, you sure are slow."

"What did you mean before about the state of her ribs?"

"They were pretty bruised. I think you forgot how strong you are in your effort to save her." Her voice was gentle, not accusing. "Mama Meod took care of them as well, don't worry."

"I didn't mean to hurt her."

"I know." She walked to the tent flap. "Watch over her for a bit, I'll be back." Then she was gone, leaving Callum, me and Haya alone together.

I waited, wondering if Callum would leave.

He didn't. He just stood there a while, staring at her.

Haya groaned, startling us both, and then shivered. By the Strings, I wished he would leave so I could comfort her, be close to her, let her know I was here.

I waited for her to call me in the spirit dimension, so I could be positive she was actually okay. But she didn't.

Callum leaned down and unlaced his boots and then stripped off his sweater. My eyes narrowed. What in the Strings was he doing?

"Come on," he whispered, lifting Haya and sliding in bed behind her, his back to the headboard. Wrapping his arms around her waist, he settled her back against him and, using his free hand he pulled the fur blanket up to her chin, effectively covering them both.

It took every ounce of my strength not to growl, not to jump out and bite his arm wrapped around her. Instead, air puffed from my nose in a short burst.

Logically I understood what he was doing. He was keeping her warm as Lev had advised. Skin to skin was the best way to do that, so I could at the least be grateful he had kept her clothes on, but come on—one night in a camp together and two rescues did not warrant such closeness between them. I had saved her countless times. It should be me holding her, keeping her warm and safe.

I sat back. What in the world was I thinking? This was

Haya. I did not own her, for all I knew she might prefer Callum with all his stocky muscle and smooth flirtations.

Who was I kidding? I watched as he tilted his head, letting hers fall gently between his neck and shoulder. They looked good together.

"Who are you?" Callum whispered against her hair, and for a moment I thought he was talking to me, when he continued, "How did you know my name?"

So Haya had called him Callum? No wonder he was all over her. Callum was from a prestigious family; even as a kid, he never gave his first name. He was always introduced by last name only. It would have been impossible for Haya to know his name. If he hadn't been suspicious of her before, he definitely was now.

He dropped his head, eyeing her lips with a look whose meaning I had learned from dark alleys and pubs. He was thinking about kissing her. Anger pulsed through my veins. The volatile nature of the emotion was surprising. I had felt the same a few times before: once with Micah, again with Callum at the camp, and later when that slave trader had assaulted her. Was this jealousy? Protectiveness? My promise to make sure she was never assaulted again burned under my skin. I wouldn't let anyone touch her like that against her will. Exposing myself to Callum mattered less than keeping that promise.

I readied myself to pounce, when Haya mumbled a single word that had both Callum and me going rigid, my blood turning to ice.

"Shroding."

CASSANDRA CIELO

FROM SAPPHIRE OCEANS

THE BODY, THE SOUL
BOOK 3

SNEAK PEEK

Chapter 1: Awakening
The Pocket Dimension

The snowy landscape chilled me to the bones, the white puffs of my breath disappearing in the growing night.

They would come, soon.

The Wraiths.

They would never stop, no matter how many we killed. I would never be safe. Even if what I hoped to accomplish came to fruition. The monsters would live on until Skithian was destroyed. The clothes Lev had given me were tattered and torn from the fight to save Coinania. Even as the Wraiths drew closer, their shadowy forms slipping towards me in the snow-laden night, I did not fear them. No, that wasn't right. Deep down I was still scared, but it wasn't my knowledge of how to kill them that had me standing on the hill unbothered. No, it was something else, something I was forgetting. Something important. Something that changed everything. What was it?

Though my mind told me I shouldn't, not with the Wraiths approaching, I folded my legs under me, sitting breezily in the snow.

"Shroding?" I whispered into the night, wanting to see him. Fear shot through my chest, not directed at the encroaching Wraiths but at the man before me.

He trudged through the snow, his loose linen tunic billowing open as he lifted his booted feet again and again. Dark gaze locked on me, rich brown locks shadowing his face from my scrutiny.

Something was not right. But what? What was so off about this encounter? Why was the wash of safety I always got in his presence evading me now?

He stalked ever closer, as if I, not the Wraiths at his back, were the enemy. Wait. The Wraiths. Why were they still here?

The night had not lifted into day; the silvery moon above was gradually turning bloodred. And though my senses were sharp, Shroding's presence showing I was in the pocket dimension, everything was all wrong.

The slide of metal, a sword being drawn, did not make any sense, until I fixed my eyes on the prince. For a fleeting second I wondered where he had gotten a sword from, but the thought was completely overridden when he poised the tip inches from my throat.

"Shroding?" I gasped, confused and afraid. He wouldn't hurt me, would he? The Wraiths were behind him—he should be fighting them. He should be protecting me. What was going on?

The side of my neck flared with pain.

"Don't you dare hide behind her," Shroding growled, his face imperious as he glared down at me.

I wanted to turn to see if there was someone else here,

behind me perhaps, but instead my body began to shake with laughter. It was a twisted sound, nothing like my own voice.

It almost sounded like... the man from the dank alley when I was a child. The man from Mama Meod's tent. A flurry of images flashed across my mind as it all came back to me.

Logan.

The Nephesh Maveth.

Right...

I was dying.

"So this is where you have been hiding, my prince." Logan spoke through me. The sensation caused bile to rise in my throat. Was this what it was like to be possessed? No, I would not be seeing this, remembering this, if it was a normal possession, and we wouldn't be in the other dimension.

"Let. Her. Go." Shroding's grip tightened on the hilt, but even with the slight shake of his hand, the blade stayed level, balanced dangerously to the curve of my neck. I was only vaguely aware it was the side Logan had bit.

"Drop the hero act, you're finished," Logan taunted. "I have you completely surrounded." My body moved, rising and standing before Shroding. Smoking Wraiths cavorted at his back, solidifying Logan's point. I wanted to warn him, to tell him to run, but my voice was not my own. "You can raise your blade all you want." He snickered as my hand flicked the tip of the sword in a mocking, unaffected gesture. "You will never hurt this body," Logan scoffed.

Shroding's hard gaze flinched, Logan's words cutting deep, before it steadied into acceptance.

"You can't come back here," Shroding warned.

What did he mean? Was he talking to me or to Logan?

He took a step forward, blade dropping as he wrapped an

arm around my shoulders, his forehead resting against mine as he sighed. "I know you are still in there."

"What are you doing?" Logan wrestled against Shroding's hold, but in my body, it was futile. I did not have the physical strength to go up against someone so much stronger, without using the gift.

"It will all be okay now, trust me."

My body jerked, but he held me firmly. I was glad I couldn't see his face. It hurt so much more than getting burned by the Wraiths. There was pressure, a searing sensation, but worst of all was the hollow cold that seeped through my core, expanding out from where the sword in Shroding's hand pierced clean through my stomach. I closed my shaking hands over his on the hilt of the blade. At my touch he let out a rattled breath that told me he was crying.

It's okay, It's okay, I thought, hoping he could hear me.

I couldn't scream, there wasn't time for it as the dimension shattered around me, and I knew then he meant I was never coming back.